MXAC

Caught Up in the Life 2

Lock Down Publications and Ca$h
Presents

Caught Up in the Life 2
A Novel by *Robert Baptiste*

Lock Down Publications
Po Box 944
Stockbridge, Ga 30281

Visit our website @
www.lockdownpublications.com

Lock Down Publications
Like our page on Facebook: Lock Down Publications @
www.facebook.com/lockdownpublications.ldp
Cover design and layout by: **Dynasty Cover Me**
Book interior design by: **Shawn Walker**
Edited by: **Jill Duska**

Stay Connected with Us!

Text **LOCKDOWN** to 22828 to stay up-to-date with new releases, sneak peaks, contests and more…

Thank you.

Submission Guideline.

Submit the first three chapters of your completed manuscript to ldpsubmissions@gmail.com, subject line: Your book's title. The manuscript must be in a .doc file and sent as an attachment. Document should be in Times New Roman, double spaced and in size 12 font. Also, provide your synopsis and full contact information. If sending multiple submissions, they must each be in a separate email.

Have a story but no way to send it electronically? You can still submit to LDP/Ca$h Presents. Send in the first three chapters, written or typed, of your completed manuscript to:

LDP: Submissions Dept
Po Box 944
Stockbridge, Ga 30281

DO NOT send original manuscript. Must be a duplicate.

Provide your synopsis and a cover letter containing your full contact information.

Thanks for considering LDP and Ca$h Presents.

Robert Baptiste

CHAPTER 1
Shantell

When we left Miami International Airport, I had a black SUV waiting for us.

When Keith was still in prison, he had told me that he wanted us to go back to Miami after he got out of prison. I love Miami as much as he does. We were considering buying a condo here for vacations.

"Damn, it feels good to be out of prison. I never thought I'd see Miami again. The last time we was here, Lebron won a championship with the Heat," Keith said.

"I still remember the game," I chimed in.

"We had a lot of fun," he continued.

"We're going to have more fun this time. We've got two weeks with no work and no kids. Just us. You know how I get down," I added.

"I can't wait," he replied.

We put our luggage in the SUV and were driven to the Fontainebleau Hotel.

I had really liked this place the first time I stayed there. I reserved a Presidential Suite with a large, golden Jacuzzi tub, a king-sized bed, servants, and all the rest of the bells and whistles you get for a thousand dollars a night. I had the whole trip planned, including a welcome home party at the Versace House. It was open to the public. It cost $60,000, and it would be a surprise for Keith for our last couple of days in town.

First, though, I was taking him to the Bal Harbour mall on the strip to shop at the designer shops. See, the feds never took the money I made from the drugs. They just wanted Deloso.

Moreover, since Eric was willing to testify, I didn't have to. I was in the clear and considering opening a couple more beauty supply stores.

"Baby, let's go. I'm going to take you shopping," I said.

"Here I come. Had to take a piss."

At Neiman Marcus, we went to the Fendi store. I bought him a couple outfits, shoes, and loafers that cost me ten grand. I spent another ten at David Yurman. Eventually, we hit Ferragamo and G Star. Altogether, I spent more than $100,000.

We left Neiman's and went to a jewelry store, where I got him a $100,000 Jacob watch and $100,000 diamond chain and earrings. I couldn't make up for the lost time, but I could make sure that he didn't want for nothing. I had made more than twenty million in drug money. It was well put up. Plus, I had a black card with no limit.

"Baby, your business must be doing really good," Keith said.

"It's doing fine."

"It must be. You're balling like a drug deala."

"Anything for my husband," I replied sweetly.

"Love you."

"I love you more." I kissed him.

Back at the hotel, we showered and dressed. We walked down to the hotel's club. It was packed wall to wall, bad bitches and fine niggas everywhere.

At the VIP section, we order some CÎROC and Patron shots. Trina and 2 Chains were in the building. The DJ had it off the chain. He was playing Cardi B's new song.

"Come on, baby. Let's hit the dance floor," I said.

I took him by the hand and led him out to the center of the dance floor. I shook my ass all over him. A couple more chicks came over to dance with us. We didn't leave until four in the morning.

Back in our room, we passed out on the bed.

I woke up later the next morning and got in the shower. Shortly after, Keith joined me there. His big black dick was hard and at attention.

"Can I join you?" he asked.

"Sure," I smiled.

We kissed. He picked me up and held me against the wall and slid his dick in my soaking wet pussy. I wrapped my legs around his waist as he drove in and out of my pussy. He kept going deeper into my walls as I came back to back. He bounced me up and down on his dick. I held his neck tightly, enjoying the ride of my life. He began to shake. Grabbing my ass cheeks, he shot his hot nut all in my soaking wet pussy.

"Damn, you got some fire pussy."

"I see you still know how to put it down on a bitch."

"You already know." He kissed me.

Later, we got dressed and hit different bars on South Beach.

***

We went to a club called Playmate. Ass was everywhere.

Fine-ass hoes were walking around butt naked, shaking their asses and giving lap dances. There were also many performing on the stages.

There were three stages in the club. On the first stage, hoes were grinding on each other. The second had fine bitches shaking their asses. The last stage had a chick putting a coke bottle in her pussy.

The club was packed from top to bottom with niggas and bitches. Keith and I went to the bar. I got $10,000 in ones and a bottle of Strawberry CÎROC. I handed him half the money as we sat down at a table where we could see all the action.

They had all kinds of nationalities in this motherfucker: Black, Puerto Rican, and Cuban, to name just a few. All of them had tattoos on their asses. Most had fake asses as well.

A high yellow, big-butted Dominican with blue hair and big titties came up to us. I noticed she was cute as she bounced her ass in my face.

"You want a lap dance?" she asked.

I nodded yes.

She sat on my lap and went to twerking all over me. I gripped her big, soft ass. This bitch was fine. I could see me and Keith tossing her ass up tonight.

"What's it going to cost me to take you home with me and my husband?"

She looked over at Keith, who was getting a lap dance from a fine light-skinned Puerto Rican and black chick. "I'll fuck you and him for free."

"You would, huh?"

"Yeah," she smiled.

"What time you get off?" I asked.

"About two," she replied.

We stayed in there until two. I spent every bit of fifty grand.

***

I watched this light-skinned, big-assed, blue-haired Dominican with tattoos all over her body bounce up and down on Keith's dick as I sucked on her red hard nipples. Keith had been asking for a threesome since he got home. It was the least I could do, considering all the shit I did while he was in jail, especially since I was keeping it a secret. So I made it happen. I'd do anything to please him. When the motherfucker asks me to jump, I don't question it. I just ask how high.

I was spooked the first couple of months after he got out. Deloso had sent me a text message threatening me and my family. But it'd been a year, and nothing had happened. I ain't going to lie. I was walking on eggshells. I had to watch my back like a motherfucka. I wondered when the hit would come, and how. I imagined getting shot, blown up, and worse.

After a while, I was like fuck it. I went back to living my life, and Keith never found out how he got out of prison.

The Dominican chick climbed off Keith and we went down on him, sucking his dick. I licked on his dick head as she sucked his balls. I climbed on top of him, and he gripped my ass cheeks, bouncing me up and down on his rock hard dick. I dug my nails into his chest as he made me cum back to back. He flipped me over and slammed his dick in my soaking wet pussy. I watched her play with her pussy.

He pulled his dick out of me and he started fucking her from the back as I kissed her all in her mouth.

"Fuck, daddy. You killing me," she said in Spanish. I watched as he thrust his dick in and out of her pussy while finger fucking her asshole. "I'm cumming." She came back to back.

He slid his dick in my asshole. I backed up on his dick as he thrust in and out of me. He gripped my ass and pulled my hair, fucking me like a dog.

"Fuck! I'm cumming!" I shouted.

"Me too," he grunted.

I slammed my ass back on his dick as he shot his hot cum into me.

"Fuck," he shouted, shaking.

"Shit, your hot cum feels good in me." I looked back and saw him biting his lip, still cumming in me. I came too. I fell on his chest. Jazz got up and went to the bathroom.

"I love you, baby," he whispered.

"I love you, too."

I thought about telling Keith everything. I needed to tell him before he found out about it in the streets. But I couldn't get a conscience. If I did, I was fucked. But I'd also be hurt if he and the kids got killed.

"Keith, I got to tell you something."

"What's up, baby?"

"Round two," Jazz said, coming back from the bathroom. She started sucking his dick.

"Fuck, yeah. Suck my dick," he moaned.

I went down on him, too. I was tripping, for real, about to get myself fucked up.

***

The Versace Villa was off the chain. It was our last day in Miami. Keith still didn't know this party was for him. We had a lot to celebrate, and I even had a big surprise for him. The DJ had the place lit. People were having a ball.

"Keith, I'll be right back."

"Where are you going?"

I didn't answer. I just walked over to the DJ and grabbed the microphone.

"Ladies and gentlemen, I want to thank y'all for coming out to celebrate with my husband and me. He just got out of the pen. He's a real stand-up guy, so that's why I threw him this party. Welcome home, baby, I love you." I blew him a kiss.

Then Mary J. came out to sing our wedding song, "Be Without You." We slow danced as we hugged and kissed each other.

"So this was your plan?" He smiled.

"You like it?"

"No. I love it."

We tongue kissed one another.

"It's the least I could do. You took care of this family for years. I just want to return the favor."

"You don't owe me anything."

"Yes, I do."

"Baby girl, I love you from the bottom of my heart, and nothing will ever change that."

I hoped to myself he meant it. If he ever found out how he got out of prison, I'd be a dead bitch.

***

Keith

I couldn't believe a nigga was out of prison, and in Miami. I love this city. I told my girl if I ever got out of prison, this was the first place I wanted to go back to.

If a motherfucker had told me that I would serve only seven years of a thirty year sentence and then get my life back with my beautiful wife and kids, I wouldn't have believed them.

God is good.

I was really blessed to have a wonderful wife that was willing to stand by me while I served thirty years. You might as well have said it was a life sentence. At thirty-five, thirty years in a USP was life.

Since I'd been home these six months, she'd blessed my

game. She'd taken me shopping, bought me a new car, and got my bank account right. She'd spent a lot of paper on a nigga and showed me mad love.

"Baby, is everything all right?" Shantell walked over to me.

"Yeah, everything is fine." I kissed her gently.

"What were you thinking about?"

"Nothing."

"You can tell me," she prodded.

"Come on, let's take a walk." I took her by the hand. We walked down the beach, watching a beautiful sunset.

"Babe, that's so pretty," she said.

"Just like you."

She kissed me. "What were you thinking about?"

"How lucky I was to have you all these years."

"Your ass sure is lucky," she replied.

"I know. You held me down."

"Love you."

"Love you back," I said as I tongue kissed her. I slid my finger into her soaking wet pussy as I undid her top with the other one. I began sucking on her hard red nipples. I laid her down on the sand and pulled her thong off. I went down, sucking and licking on her swollen red pearl tongue.

"Yes, baby, eat this pussy. I'm cumming!" She pulled my head down as she came in my face. "Keith, I love you."

I slid my hard dick into her pussy as she held me close, tongue kissing me. I thrust in and out of her as she dug her nails into my back.

"I love you, Shantell."

"I love you, Keith."

She got on top of me and rode me like a horse. I grabbed her cheeks, thrusting dick in and out of her.

"Fuck. I'm cumming," she said, shaking.

"Me, too," I said, shaking and shooting all my nut in her as she came again. She laid on top of my chest as we watched the sunset.

Robert Baptiste

CHAPTER 2
Eric

"Eric Hampton, get ready for court."

As I heard the CO on the speaker, I got up and put on my orange jumpsuit and white Nikes. I was currently being held in a federal detention center in Houston, Texas. The feds had me tied into a conspiracy with this motherfucker Deloso. The feds had already extradited Deloso to New Orleans. That bitch Shantell had been working for the feds in New Orleans. The feds were accusing me of conspiracy to distribute a thousand kilograms of cocaine, as well as engaging in cartel murders.

As I left my cell, the CO patted me down and put me in leg shackles and handcuffs.

As we got off the elevator, he led me to a white van, where ten other federal inmates were waiting to make the trip to the federal court. As the federal marshals drove us to the court building, I started thinking. I still couldn't believe I was caught up in this shit because of that bitch Shantell.

My life had been good. I was balling, fucking nothing but bad bitches, and traveling when I wanted. Thanks to Brittney's bitch ass for introducing me to her bitch-ass, snitching friend. I was fucked. Come to find out, the bitch did it to get her husband out of prison. Now I'm looking at life, and the feds have a hundred witnesses waiting to testify against me.

I was not going to take a life sentence for nobody. Fuck that. The feds were offering me a deal to cooperate. I wanted to hear what they had to say.

The federal building in Houston was an imposing, white structure in downtown Houston. The marshals put me in the holding cell by myself. Ten minutes later, a black U.S. marshal took me upstairs to the round table.

The round table was where deals were made. Once there, you either chose to cooperate or you didn't. But by the time you reach this room, you're already cooperating.

I sat in a black leather chair next to my lawyer as we awaited the prosecutor. I had the best lawyer in Houston. I had paid him $100,000 to get me the best deal he could.

After about ten minutes, a slim white lady, whose long blonde hair was tied in a ponytail, came in and laid some folders on the table.

"My name is Mary Brown. I'm the prosecutor on this case. I'm working with the federal district attorney's office in New Orleans. Your lawyer said you wanted a deal. Is this correct?"

"Yes, it is."

"What do you want?" she asked.

My lawyer answered, "My client wants immunity for all charges."

"I don't know. We will need a guilty plea, and will offer a three hundred sixty month sentence."

"Thirty years is essentially a life sentence. My client is thirty-six years old."

"We have others who are willing to testify."

"They don't know what my client knows. He's your star witness."

"It has to be really good. These charges are too serious for him just to go free."

"It is," I said.

My attorney added, "We got a deal or not?"

"I'll need to know what information you have."

My attorney nodded, and I said, "The federal agent that came up missing several years ago...I know where his body's buried at."

The ADA and the agents rushed from the room. Ten minutes later, they came back with the agreement. My lawyer read the document, and told me to sign it.

I signed.

"Now, where's the agent's body?" the ADA asked.

"He's buried in Monticello, Texas, in the desert. I can draw you a map to the location."

"Is this him?" She passed me a picture.

I looked at the white agent in his uniform. It was the one I'd helped Deloso cut up and bury. It was how I gained Deloso's trust. It was a way for me to get in the Gulf Coast Family.

"Yeah, that's him."

"You sure his body is there?"

"I'm positive."

My attorney said, "Look, y'all need to move my client to a safe location."

"We're working on it."

Back at the county jail, I was packing my stuff to move. When you're cooperating, you never know who is connected to whom, so you can get killed at any time. I had to go into witness protection until this trial shit was over. Harris County had too many Mexicans. I didn't trust it here.

As I was grabbing my things, two bald, tattooed Mexicans ran into my cell. I knocked the first one down, but three more were coming, all stabbing me with shanks.

I fell to the floor with blood coming from everywhere. I tried to crawl out of the cell and scream for help, but everyone on the tier was just watching. In jail, a rat don't get no love. It was no secret that when you're talking to the feds, everyone knows. Even if the guys wanted to help me, they couldn't. They didn't want to be connected to a rat. In the feds, it followed you everywhere. They kept stomping me until I lost consciousness.

The last thing I heard was, "This is from Deloso, motherfucker."

The guard ran in and pepper sprayed them. They laid on the floor, their shanks still beside them. But it was too late.
I had lost too much blood. I said a brief prayer. The damage was done. I took my last breath lying in a pool of my own blood on a cold concrete floor.

Robert Baptiste

CHAPTER 3
Sandra

I was in my office putting together the case against Deloso and the Gulf Coast Cartel. This case had potential. It might even help me achieve my goal of becoming mayor of New Orleans. It was the biggest case my office had ever had. I'd gotten this case based on my fifteen years of experience as a federal prosecutor. It had to be a slam dunk if I wanted it to help me.

I had more than a hundred witnesses. I even had an informant close to Deloso in Houston. He had just revealed where a murdered agent was buried. We were about to get him back here to testify.

Winning this case would look good on my resume. I could see it now: Sandra Lewis. The first African American woman to run for and win the New Orleans mayor's office. That had a nice ring to it.

My thoughts were interrupted as one of the prosecutors came into my office. He looked stunned. I was only an ADA, but this was my case, and I had several attorneys and interns helping with this case.

"What the hell is wrong with you? You forgot to knock."

He put the folder on the desk as he tried to catch his breath.

"What's this?" I asked, opening the folder. I saw a picture of my witness dead on the floor of the Harris County jail.

"That's Eric Hampton. He's our key informant in this case," Adam said.

"I know who he is. What happened to him?"

"He was killed in an incident involving a number of Mexican inmates. Deloso must have sent a hit on him."

"Shit! Shit! Shit!" I stood up and rubbed my hands over my head. "Our star witness is gone, and the trial starts in seven days."

"We still have the agent's body that we found in the desert."

"We needed Hampton to link him to the murder."

"We have more than a hundred witnesses to testify against him."

"A few worked for Deloso, but there are some credibility issues."

"What about the woman who set him up?"

"Shantell?"

"She worked undercover to arrest him."

"But we made a deal that she wouldn't have to testify so that her husband would never find out."

"So you're going to trial and taking a chance on him getting off? All we got are some low level workers and some professional informants from prison saying they bought drugs from him."

"The jury will see the evidence and convict him."

"Are you sure? You know he's coming with the best attorneys money can buy. He'll walk like John Gotti did."

"Adam, we can't go back on our deal. It would keep others from helping. They would think we will renege on their deal, too. That's not a good look."

"Letting this cartel head off wouldn't be a good look either. Besides, it wasn't your deal. The last prosecutor made it."

"You're right. You'll be a good prosecutor. Get out, and let me think a minute."

I looked out the big window in my office at Canal Street. If I broke this deal, it could stop others from coming to us. On the other hand, if this motherfucka Deloso walked, I'd be fucked. My career would go down the drain. I could kiss the mayor's office goodbye. My star witness was dead. Those motherfuckers were too dumb to put him in witness protection.

"The FDA in Texas on line one," my secretary said.

"Pass her through," I replied. "Hello."

"I'm sure you've heard."

"Yeah, it puts a big hole in my case. Why wasn't he in witness protection?"

"We were setting it up."

"Shit!"

"What are you going to do?"

"I have to get in touch with someone who was close to the case and hope she will help."

"Who is this person?"

"I'll keep it to myself for now."

"Good luck. Sorry again. Keep me posted."

"Will do."

I hoped Shantell was willing to play. I hated to have to put a move on her, but I needed her to come through. I couldn't let this case get away from me and fuck up my chances to become the mayor.

I dialed her number.

Robert Baptiste

CHAPTER 4
Shantell

We got to our new house in Metairie on the outskirts of New Orleans. I wanted to get out of the city because I didn't need people coming up to talk about drugs when I was hanging out with Keith. I wanted to leave the past behind me. So I went to Cherokee Avenue in the suburbs before Keith got out of prison. I sold our house in Eastover and bought this one for 1.2 million. I told Keith I had expanded my beauty supply stores to other states, one in Houston and the other in Atlanta.

The new house is large. It's white stone with a big pool and an attached two-car garage. It has five bedrooms and six bathrooms with more than four thousand square feet of living space. The house sits on an oversized 60 x150 lot. There is a grand entrance with curved stairs, a large formal dining room, and a nearby butler's pantry and wet bar. The kitchen has marble floors and countertops. The Subzero appliances are all stainless steel. There is also a large breakfast nook. We have a master suite and a guest bedroom along with three more bedrooms, each connecting to a balcony that overlooks the pool. There is also a media room and an office with its own private balcony. There is a cabana that serves as a guest house in the back with a kitchen, a full bath, and an entry at poolside.

"Baby, did you enjoy the last two weeks?" I asked while smiling at him.

"Yeah, thank you for it. It's one of the reasons I love you." He kissed me.

"I love you back."

"I'll get the bags."

As I entered the house, the phone rang. I recognized the number, but didn't answer. I didn't have time to deal with that bullshit. My life was great. I wasn't going to fuck that up for nobody.

The kids ran up. "Y'all back! What did y'all bring us?"

"Hey to y'all, too."

"Hey, y'all." Keith Jr. and Ka'wine hugged us.

"That's more like it."

"Now, what did y'all bring us?"

I handed them a collection of bags we had gotten for them. They quickly looked inside and then ran upstairs.

"Dinner will be ready shortly!" I screamed.

Damn, the kids are growing up fast. When all this started, Ka'wine was eight and Keith Jr. was ten. Now they're teenagers, sixteen and eighteen. Shit, Ka'wine's breasts are bigger than mine, and Keith Jr. is almost as tall as his daddy.

My phone rang again. *Those Fed motherfuckers starting this bullshit again. I'm just not up to it. Fuck whatever they want. I did my part,* I thought as I let the phone go to voicemail.

CHAPTER 5
Shantell
Three weeks later

I was lying on Keith's chest. We were each trying to catch our breath after hot, sweaty sex. Since we'd gotten back from Miami, all we'd been doing was fucking like rabbits, trying to make another baby. Both of us wanted another child. My life was running smoothly. My kids were about to graduate. Keith wanted to reopen his business. Best of all, he didn't know shit.

I had told Jackie, Ke'shon, Icy, and Brittany not to run their fucking mouths to Keith about anything we did while he was locked up. Those hoes still didn't know what I did to get him home. They didn't even know they had been working for the Feds. It was my little secret, and I planned to keep it that way. Even Baldwin, our lawyer, had been playing his role. He was keeping his mouth shut.

Meanwhile, I'd been at home, playing the good wife, fucking and sucking Keith to death, just like a good little bitch is supposed to do. I hoped he never found out what I did while he was in prison.

My phone rang. It was the Feds again. Those bitches had been trying to talk to me ever since we'd gotten back from Miami. I still didn't know why. I had made a deal. Once my husband came home, I was done. They told me I was free.

I knew that Eric and a hundred other witness were lined up to testify. They certainly didn't need me on the stand. I was happy that way.

If Keith ever found out about that shit, I'd be a dead bitch. I don't know why they kept calling me. I didn't have shit for them. I was certainly not trying to get involved in anything else the Feds had going on. I'd put in my work for the government, and we both won.

"Who's that calling you? They've called a hundred times since we've been in bed," Keith asked.

"Jackie's ass." *Let me answer this bitch before those hoes come knocking at my motherfucking door*, I thought. I certainly didn't need that. I got out of bed, grabbing my phone.

"Baby, where are you going?"

"To use the bathroom. Be right back."

"Hurry back. I'm getting hard again."

In the bathroom, I turned on the sink and sat on the toilet. I really had to piss. Keith was beating a bitch's bladder up.

I called the FDA office. I was transferred to a woman who began without hesitation. "Ms. Washington, we have a problem."

"We don't got shit."

"Yes, we do. Eric Hampton was killed in prison."

"So? What does that have to do with me?"

"We need your testimony."

"Oh, hell no! You told me I wasn't going to have to do that. We made a deal."

"Things change. You're the best witness we have left."

"Man, y'all tripping right now. I was getting some dick, and you call me for this bullshit. I'm not about to let my husband find out how he got out. My life is straight. Sorry, I can't help you."

"If you don't, your family could face a big problem."

"Whatever." I hung up the phone.

I got off the toilet and went back to bed. My husband was stroking his dick, getting it hard.

"What did Jackie want?"

"Some money," I said, going down on him, swallowing his whole dick.

Later, I got up to check my messages. It was horrifying: YOU BLACK BITCH. YOU THINK IT'S OVER? IT'S NEVER OVER. I TOLD YOU NOT TO FUCK ME OVER. NOW KEITH, YOUR KIDS, AND YOU ARE DEAD. THIS IS JUST THE BEGINNING.

My heart pounded. My head was fucked up. I ran to the bathroom to throw up. How could this motherfucker have my number? His ass was in prison. *Fuck, what have I done now?* I wondered.

I walked back to the bedroom and saw that Keith was

sleeping. I wanted to wake him up and tell him everything. But he wouldn't understand. He would probably kill my ass.

I'd fucked up now. I'd gotten my family in some deep shit. FUCK!

***

I was in the shower letting the hot water run over my body.
I was thinking about what the prosecutor had told me. Deloso would get out of prison if I didn't testify. *If this motherfucker goes free, my whole family is dead,* I thought.

There was no telling what that crazy motherfucker would do to them. I had seen him do psycho shit to people. I watched him butcher and bury an entire family in the desert. Their bodies still hadn't been found. He had beaten a DEA agent to death with a baseball bat right in front me.

The Feds couldn't protect me. Eric was being held in protective custody, and Deloso had still found a way to kill his ass. I knew Deloso had a hit out on my family. This shit was hitting me hard.

Keith didn't have a clue what was going on, and I couldn't bring myself to tell him. My poor husband thought he got out of prison by winning his appeal. But I was not ready to face that music. I couldn't tell him yet. I'd cross that bridge when I got there. My life was good right now. I couldn't mess that up.

I had my family back. Keith and I were working on another baby. Keith and I had been having the best life. We'd had a few threesomes with Icy. She was still my side bitch. I was still looking out for her.

Keith pulled the curtain back. He was butt naked with his long, black, nine-inch dick rock hard in his hand. He was smiling, "Can I join you?"

"Sure."

"You look like you got something on your mind."

"I'm fine." I put on my best fake smile.

"You know you can talk to me about anything. Right?" He got

in the shower and stared straight into my eyes.

"I know. It's all good." I began stroking his dick as I kissed him. I was hoping he wouldn't ask a lot of questions.

He picked me up and slid his dick in my wet pussy. He pinned me to the wall and started fucking the shit out of me.
I dug my fingers into his back as I came all over his dick. He went even deeper in my pussy, slamming his dick in my pussy walls as he shot his hot nut into my pussy.

"Fuck! I love you," I said as we kissed.

"I love you too."

***

After we made love in the shower, I felt so bad that I wanted to cry. This man genuinely loved me and would've given me the world, but I was sitting here holding back a lie from him. Worse, I'd put his life in danger.

I got dressed and jumped in my white G wagon. I needed a break from all the madness that I had created. I had to get away. If this kept up, I was going to have to tell him. A bitch gets real emotional and sentimental when he puts it down and has a bitch cumming back to back. A bitch will get to spilling all the beans about herself.

As I rode around, a million thoughts flew through my head. I didn't know what to do. If I didn't testify, Deloso would get out of prison and kill my family. And I was fucked.

If I testified, he'd have people kill my family. And I'd still be fucked. So I had twelve in one hand, and a dozen in the other. I needed a plan, fast. I was praying they would find a new witness. I could lose my husband over this shit. He'd told me not to fuck with it. But I wouldn't listen. Now, I was stuck between a rock and a hard place.

My phone rang. I answered.

"Have you thought about what I said, Ms. Washington?"

"I told you. I'm not fucking with that."

"But –"

Before she could finish, I hung up. I wished these motherfuckers would stop calling me. I couldn't even think clearly. They'd been calling back to back, every hour, on the hour, working on my nerves.

My phone rang again. It was Jackie.

"Hey, baby," I started.

"You still coming down for the party?"

"I don't know."

"Bitch! Let the dick breathe."

"Fuck you, hoe."

"I need you here for the opening of my new salon."

"Okay, I'll be there."

"Thanks. It's this Friday."

"I'll get a flight out tomorrow."

"Good. Everybody's coming."

"Good. One big happy family."

"Yeah."

"I'll call when I get there."

I needed to tell them what was going on, but I wasn't sure they needed to know the truth. It would freak them out, and they would run their mouths. It might get back to Keith.

I needed to figure out what to do.

Robert Baptiste

CHAPTER 6
Keith

I got out of the black Bentley coupe that my girl bought me when I came home. I was so proud of her for holding shit down while I was in prison. She had opened a couple more beauty supply stores. They were doing well.

Our lovemaking had been out of sight. A nigga was getting so much pussy that he couldn't even breathe. Plus, Shantell had been freakier than she was before I went to prison.

I had been home a couple of months and I needed to try to open my construction company back up.

I walked into Baldwin's law firm, and the receptionist greeted me.

"Can I help you?" she asked.

"I'm here to see Baldwin."

"Your name?"

"Keith Washington."

"Have a seat. I'll let Mr. Baldwin know you're here."

I sat on a black leather couch and looked around. Baldwin had come up since I went to prison. He had bought his own building in Slidell, on the outskirts of New Orleans.

There was a large receptionist desk built out of cherry wood, two black leather couches, and big glass windows. His name was written in large, black letters on the door. He had a few billboards around the city. He also had a big sexy yellow-bone secretary, whose ass was perfectly fitting the yellow skirt she was wearing.

"Mr. Washington, Mr. Baldwin will see you."

"Okay."

I followed her to the back while I checked out the secretary's round fat ass. I wouldn't mind having a threesome with her. I was a sucker for yellow and red bones.

When I entered his office, Baldwin got up from behind his glass desk. He was in a black Armani suit with gator shoes on. He'd gained a little weight.

"I'm glad to see you're out. How have you been?"

"Man, I'm glad I'm out that bitch too. But I'm doing real good. I see you've moved up in the world."

"Yeah, business is great. I have no complaints. Have a seat. What brings you by?"

"It's really nice in here. You have a big fish tank, glass desk with brown leather chairs, and a fine-ass secretary."

"Yes, everything is good. Now what do you need?"

"First, I need you to get the money from my overseas account. There should be about $1.2 million."

"No problem. It'll take a couple of days."

"Also, I want to reopen my construction company."

"Do you have a location in mind?"

"I'm looking into a few things."

"Let me know. I will make it happen. I know some people. We can probably get you a loan."

"Thanks. That's all I need."

"Sound like a plan. How are the wife and kids?"

"Fine. Everything is everything. It feels good not to have to look over my shoulder."

"I know that's right."

"I'm going to take a ride around the city. Everything is different."

"It sure is, since you went to prison. This motherfucker is the new New Orleans."

"I hear you. I'm out."

He walked around the table to hug me before I left his office.

***

Baldwin

After Keith left, I sat down in my chair, rubbing my head.

I hoped he never found out how he got out of prison. There would be hell to pay. I hoped his dumb-ass wife didn't get emotional and tell everything. If she did, and if Keith found out I was part of it, he would kill my ass.

I needed to talk to Shantell about this money, because I'd

spent the $1.2 million Keith was talking about, so her ass was going to give me some of those millions the Feds let her keep. Plus, Keith was going to need more than $1.2 million to restart his business. He'd need close to five. It's hard to get $5 million when you're fresh out of jail.

As I thought about calling Shantell, my phone rang.

"May I speak to Mr. Baldwin?" a woman's voice answered.

"This is he. Who are you?"

"I'm Sandra Lewis. I'm the lead prosecutor in the Deloso trial."

My heart skipped a beat when she said his name. Keith's wife had busted him. I thought she was out of this shit. "How can I help you?"

"I've been trying to contact Ms. Washington. We need her to testify against Deloso."

"I thought you agreed that she didn't have to testify."

"Our primary witness was killed. We need her testimony, or Deloso walks."

"Her deal with you said that her husband wouldn't know any of this. How will this work if she testifies?"

"If Deloso walks, her family and yours will be endangered."

"My life? What do you mean?"

"That's how the cartel works. They kill everyone who played a role in their arrest. Your name will be on their hit list as well."

"I didn't do anything."

"You're connected to Ms. Washington. You need to help us get her to testify."

"Let me get back with you."

I was fucked. The cartel would come after me for helping Shantell. But when Keith found out, he'd kill my ass. I slammed my hand against my desk. I knew I should have never gotten involved in this. I had a feeling it was bad news. This shit was going to get me killed just because I was trying to be a good friend.

I picked up the phone, calling Shantell.

***
Keith

I rode around the city. It was amazingly different since I had been locked up. As I rode down MLK, I saw that the city had torn down the projects and replaced it with some nice Section 8 housing. It was fenced and the police patrolled the area now. There were Section 8 houses where the Calliope used to be.

I used to make a lot of money in the projects. That was where I came up: hustling, jacking, and killing. Those projects gave a nigga a lot of game and taught me how to make it in the streets of New Orleans. They were hard lessons, but I became a boss in the city and ran it for a while.

Even looking back today, I wouldn't change anything. The streets made me the man I am today.

My phone rang.

"Nigga, where you at?" a male voice rumbled.

"I'm on my way. Wanted to sightsee."

"I'm pulling up to Anita's now."

"On my way."

"One."

I rode down Tulane to Anita's, one of my favorite restaurants. It had the best food in the city, besides Jean's.

As I pulled up, my man Brad was waiting outside, leaning on his black Benz. Brad was black as midnight with cat eyes and a bald head. He was one of my right-hand men, but nobody knew him. I used him to kidnap motherfuckers to bring them to me. He was a cold killer. He could get anybody I wanted him to.

He still messed around in the streets from time to time.

We had grown up in together in the projects. He was my best friend. When I left the game, I made sure he was taken care of. When I went to prison, I left him a million dollars so he could invest it for me. Plus, he looked out for me when I was in prison. He was a true friend. He was the one that I told to send my girl the money.

I got out of my car, and we hugged.

"Man, you look good," he said.

"Nigga, you don't look half bad yourself.

"I'm glad you're home."

"Me too."

"Come on. Let's go in."

We sat in a booth and ordered breakfast.

"Can I take y'all order?" a slim black older waitress asked.

"Yes, I would like grits, sausage, and sunny-side up eggs. Oh, and some orange juice," I said.

"Same for me," Brad added.

"Coming up."

"So how does it feeling being out?"

"Man, it's a blessing."

"That bitch-ass nigga told on you."

"It fucked me up."

"I knew that nigga was a hoe. I used to tell you all the time, but you took up for the nigga. He was too thirsty to take over."

"You're right. I can't argue about that."

"What's good with the wife and kids?"

"Man, things are good."

"So what are you going to do now?"

The waitress brought our food to the table.

"I'm trying to reopen my construction business."

"I got money for you."

"Leave it where it's at. I'm trying to get a bank loan."

"Let me know if you need anything. I got you."

"I know. It's all love."

We chilled in Anita's, talking, playing catch up.

"Man, the city changed like a motherfucker," I said.

"Yeah, white people moved in after Katrina and bought up everything."

"I see. What are you into these days?"

"I'm in the real estate game. I buy and sell houses all over the city."

"You still in the streets?"

"I'm never out. I keep my ears to the streets."

"Let's go. I got to push."
"Alright."
We dapped and hugged.
"Holla at me," he called.
"You know I will."

***

Shantell

I walked into the Copeland restaurant on St. Charles, looking around for Baldwin. He'd called and told me that he needed to talk to me about something. I didn't have a clue as to what it could be. Everything was going smoothly on my end.

He flagged me to the table, and pulled out my chair for me.
"Thanks. Now, what is this about?"
"I'm glad you could make it."
"You said you needed to talk. It sounded serious."
"Keith came to see me today?"
"For what? You kept your mouth closed, right?"
"Yes, but it was not for that."
"What was it for?"
"His money."
"Money?"
"Yes. Before he went to prison, he gave me 1.2 million."
"So what that got to do with me?"
"I need your help."
"What for?"
"Because I don't have it."
"What you mean you don't have it? You making money."
"I spent it on upgrading my office, and other stuff."
"Well, you need to find it."
"Look, I need you to cut me a check. I know the Feds didn't take all the money. Plus I haven't told Keith shit."
"So you blackmailing me?"
"It's not like that. I just need your help, like you need mine."
"So that's how it is?"

36

"No. Do you want Keith to go back to jail?"

"Keith not going nowhere."

"Yes, he is, after he finds out I don't have his money. He's going to kill my ass."

I locked eyes with him. I thought about what he said. "Okay, but once I give you this money, we are fucking through. Don't call me for shit. I'm serious."

"Thank you. And there's one more thing I need to tell you."

"Kiss my ass. We through." I walked out.

I jumped in my car, pissed off. I couldn't believe this motherfucker was blackmailing me.

Robert Baptiste

CHAPTER 7
Shantell
Two months later

As I was leaving Wal-Mart, my phone rang.

"You black bitch. Do you think you can get away from me? I'm going to kill your family," a deep bass voice said.

I looked around to try to see if someone was following me. As I got in my car, my heart was pounding. My phone rang again. It was Keith.

"Hey, baby," I started, trying to sound normal.

"I was just calling to see if you wanted me to pick up something to eat?"

"I'm just leaving Wal-Mart with some food for dinner tonight."

"Are you okay? You sound different."

"I'm fine. Dumbass at the light. Just a little upset."

"Be careful. I'll see you at the house."

As I hung up, a thousand thoughts were racing through my mind. I knew that motherfucker was still in jail.

When I got home, Keith was watching the news. Deloso was the lead story. It was a shot of him in handcuffs. They said he had supplied lots of drugs to New Orleans and much of the South. It also talked about how many people he had killed.

"Keith, are you going to help me in the kitchen?" I wanted to get him in the kitchen before they discussed the trial and all of the people who were connected to him.

"I'll be there in a minute."

I was nervous as I started putting up the food. I hoped and prayed they wouldn't mention my name. As I heard the TV cut off, my stomach was turning like I had to take a shit.

As Keith came in, I was putting a chicken in the oven. I was trying to avoid eye contact.

"Baby, you know they have my old connect in federal custody?" Keith said.

"What?" I still avoided looking at him.

"Yeah, that shit had my stomach in a knot. I hope them motherfuckers don't come after me now and try to put me in a conspiracy with him. Another jail sentence will be hard to swallow. You know a nigga will stand up, but I don't want to leave y'all again."

"And we don't want you to leave us either," I said, stirring the Kool-Aid.

"I wonder how he got busted. It had to be somebody close to him. Trial starts on March 3rd. He's looking at life."

"For real?" I walked over to the stove.

"Yeah. I'll tell you what, whoever did it, their whole family is dead."

The more he talked, the tenser my stomach became.

"This motherfucker won't stop until he gets them. I know how he operates. Cross him, and your light is put out. He won't stop until their whole family is dead, as well as anyone who is close to them. That's why I didn't rat on this motherfucker. He probably has already ordered the hit from jail. That shit can't hold him."

"Call the kids down. It's time for supper." I was holding my stomach.

"You okay?"

"My stomach's a little bit upset. I need to go to the restroom."

He called the kids as I sat on the toilet with my nerves bad as a motherfucker. My legs were shaking and diarrhea was coming out of my ass. Even though I don't smoke, I wished I had a cigarette.

I took a hard hit on a blunt as I thought about what Keith had said. He had my head fucked up. I knew he wasn't lying. He had worked for the motherfucker. I had seen Deloso operate firsthand. I had to figure this shit out fast. I needed to make that trip to Atlanta to free my mind. Right now, I was stressed the fuck out.

"Baby girl, you alright?"

"I'm fine."

"I put your food in the microwave."

"Thanks. I'll be out in a second."

I sprayed some air freshener as I got in the shower. After finishing, I wrapped my towel around myself and went to the bedroom. Keith was on the bed, watching SportsCenter. I got in bed and put my head on his chest.

"You alright?" he asked, rubbing his hand through my hair.

"Everything's good. Jackie's having a party for her new shop. I'm going to Atlanta."

"Okay, no problem."

"I love you." I kissed him as I climbed on top of him, unzipped his pants, and slid his dick into my warm, wet pussy.

"Fuck, I need this." I rode him like a horse.

"Yeah, baby, ride this dick." He bounced me up and down on his dick.

I came all over his dick as he thrust deeper into me. He flipped me over and put my legs on his shoulders as he went deeper and harder into my walls.

I dug my nails into his back. I enjoyed every minute of it. I was coming back to back as he started to shake.

"I'm about to nut," he said.

I wrapped my legs around him and held his ass cheeks tight as he shot his warm nut into my pussy. We tongue kissed.
He rolled over as I lay my head on his chest.

"Shantell, I love you. And I want to thank you for holding a nigga down while I was away."

"It's all good. You're my husband. I did what any wife would do for her man.

"I know, but you could have left and moved on with your life. You could have taken the kids and I'd never have seen them again."

The more he talked, the more my conscience started bothering me. He was breaking down my walls. He had my pussy soaking wet. When a bitch gets some good dick, her emotions start to get involved. I needed to stay strong, but it was hard.

He was playing with my hair and telling me how much he loved me. He slid his dick back in me, looking deep into my eyes, like he could see my soul.

"Shantell, I'm truly in love with you. I want to give you the world."

"Keith, I need to tell you something."

He pulled out a diamond necklace from under his pillow and put it on my neck.

"I love you."

"It's beautiful. And I love you back."

"Now, what did you want to say?"

"That I love you. I'm glad you're home."

"Same here."

We tongue kissed as he slowly stroked me.

CHAPTER 8
Shantell

I left the airport and felt Atlanta's heat. It hit me like a sledgehammer. The heat there was worse than New Orleans.

Jackie was waiting for me, leaning on a red Bentley coupe. She had on a yellow and blue sundress with yellow Chanel sandals. Her hair was short and dyed blue. Her lipstick, fingernails, and toes matched. The bitch was still fine as hell.

We hugged one another and kissed each other's cheeks.

"I'm glad you came, bitch," Jackie announced with a smirk.

"I wasn't going to come," I honestly replied.

"Like that, huh?" she asked, and then added, "Looks like you've gained some weight."

"Eating and fucking will do that to you." I giggled.

"I see you got that glow going on," she said.

"So how has the A been treating you?" I changed the subject to get the attention off of me.

"The men are loving my body. You like?" She spun around.

"Looks like you got your ass done," I commented.

"Titties, too," Jackie replied.

"Baby got back." I slapped her ass.

"You already know."

"But you had ass already."

"Shit, in the A, that's what these niggas like. These niggas are used to them thick-ass strippers with their fat asses."

"Whatever. Let's get out this heat."

"Let's go."

As we started for her house, I said, "The salon must be taking off for you."

"That's why I wanted you to come. I'm celebrating opening my third salon. And in less than a year."

"I'm happy for you."

Her house was white and looked like a small mansion.

"I see you're doing well in the A."

"A little something. Everything is cheaper here than back

home."

"Me and Keith are thinking about building a house here. You know, since I got my other supply store here."

"Bitch, y'all should. You can be my neighbor. Make sure you build in Buckhead. It's cheaper here on the outskirts of the city."

"That's good to know."

"It'll be like old times. Running the streets and hitting clubs up and turning bitches out. They got some bad ones up here."

"I've heard."

"Let me show you the house."

She had hardwood floors throughout. Her living room had white leather couches and armchairs and a 50-inch TV hanging on the wall. Her kitchen had white and gray marble counters and floors and stainless steel appliances in the middle. She had white carpet running up the stairs to connect to the six bedrooms upstairs.

"This is my room." She opened a door.

She had an oversized, king-sized bed with blue sheets and a white bedspread. Her floors were covered in thick white carpet. She had a curved 50-inch TV on the wall, a mirror on the ceiling, and a balcony overlooking her pool.

"A mirror?"

"Bitch, you know I'm a freak. I like to watch myself getting fucked."

Back downstairs, we walked outside. She had a large pool and patio.

"How much you pay for this house?" I asked.

"$900,000," she casually replied.

"I like it," I commented.

"Thanks. Let's go to the living room, have a drink, and play catch-up. I'm waiting for the rest of these bitches to show up."

"You got some weed?" I inquired.

"I got you."

I sat on the couch. She came back with strawberry Ciroc and two blunts.

"Here," she said, handing me the bottle.

I poured drinks as she lit the blunt. She took a puff and then passed it to me. I took a hard hit and started choking.

"Bitch, this ain't no regular weed. It's black widow," she said, patting me on the back as I choked.

"Shit, this stuff is killer," I replied, still choking.

As we talked, I heard a knock at the door.

"Who is it?" Jackie asked.

"Me, bitch," Ke'shon said.

She came in wearing green leggings, a matching halter top, and white Air Max. Her hair was dyed red and short. She had gotten a tummy tuck and put the fat in her ass, which was big and round like a stripper's. She was also running my store out here.

"I see you got some work done," I said as we hugged and kissed.

"You like?" She turned around.

"ATL got you hoes turned out," I commented.

"That's what it's about down here: ass," Ke'shon retorted.

"I tried to tell her that," Jackie added.

"Well, you look good," I said.

"So do you. I've missed you," she said.

Jackie took us back into the living room to talk.

"So what have you been up to?" I asked.

"Nothing. Just living the single life. Fucking who I want," she chuckled.

"That's good. I thought you were going to open a club?" I inquired.

"I'm working on it. I'm trying to get permits in order."

"If you need any help, let me know."

"I will. What's up with you and Keith?" she asked.

"Shit, fucking like rabbits. We just got back from Miami."

"I heard that. Bitch, I thought your ass would be pregnant by now," Ke'shon announced.

"Shit, I was surprised she wasn't already," Jackie added.

There was another knock on the door. Jackie answered and Brittney's fine ass walked in.

"Hey, bitches," she said, hugging us.

She had on a red halter with red leggings. Her hair was cut short and dyed blonde. The bitch was still fine, with a big ass and big fake titties.

"What's up, stranger? Long time, no see," she said.

"I've been busy," I replied.

"I see you got that glow. Keith must be dropping that dick on you on the regular."

"You already know," I responded. Then I added, "What are we going to do tonight in Hotlanta? I came to turn up in this bitch, to suck some pussy and dick."

"Well, you ain't said a word. We can hit up some clubs," Jackie said.

"Good, because I haven't been to Magic City. I want to see them fine, big butt hoes," Brittney answered.

"Well, I see it will be like old times," I said.

"I'll toast to that," Jackie said as we tapped our glasses together.

***

Magic City was packed. Jackie knew some people and got us into the VIP. It was a lot like KOD in Miami: butt-naked bitches running around everywhere, giving niggas lap dances or twerking, and busting it open on the stage. I'm talking big fine, black, corn-fed bitches with big asses. Some were fake, but many were real.

We went to the bar and got $10,000 in ones and ordered Ciroc and Patron shots. We sat at the table in front of the stage, watching the hoes bust it open as we threw ones at them.

A couple of strippers came by. "Do y'all want lap dances?" a dark-skinned chick with tattoos all over her body asked.

"Hell yeah," we answered.

They started twerking and shaking their asses in our faces and on our laps. Before long, there was a flock of hoes surrounding us, twerking and busting their pussies open for us.

Jackie had given us some molly pills at her house, so we were super high and horny. We left at 3 a.m. and took the party back to

Jackie's house. We took five bad-ass strippers with us.

It was a big orgy at Jackie's. Everybody was fucking and sucking each other. Brittney had a fine redbone with long red hair. Ke'shon had a fine black chick with long gold weave. Jackie had a brown-skinned bitch with short pink hair. I had a fine high yellow bitch with short blue hair and a butterfly tattoo on her ass. We took turns eating each other out.

Now, this what a vacation was supposed to be. I needed this shit to take my mind off what was going on in New Orleans with this Fed shit.

Just like old times, I thought.

***

I got up the next morning and looked around the living room. Pussy and ass were everywhere. I grabbed my phone and checked my messages as I went to the bathroom.

I had missed a few calls from Keith and the kids. Both Baldwin and the prosecutor had called, but I didn't have time for that bullshit. They wanted me to testify against Deloso. But I'd put in my work. I was not fucking with anything else.

I called Keith. He answered on the first ring.

"I just want to make sure you got there. You didn't call."

"I'm sorry. I got caught up with the girls. Is everything okay? The kids called too."

"Everything's fine."

"I'll be home in a couple of days."

"Love you."

"Love you back."

I got in the shower, and the prosecutor crossed my mind. They wanted me on that stand against Deloso.

I had already risked my life setting him up. I should have never gotten in bed with those motherfuckers. Once you're in, they won't let you out.

I got out of the shower and into my yellow sundress and white L.V. sandals. It was too hot for makeup or panties, so I went natural with my hair in a bun.

I went to see the MLK house and 2pac's school. I had never seen it. I wanted to see Atlanta for myself before any of those hoes got up, especially since Keith and I were considering building a house here. I grabbed the keys to Jackie's Land Rover and drove to MLK's house. There was a long line of people since it was his birthday weekend. Then I went to the underground mall to do some shopping. I ran into a couple of celebrities and got a picture.

As I got back in the truck, Jackie called. "Bitch, how in the fuck you just going to leave us here? Where are you at?"

"Coming out of the mall."

"Bring us some McDonald's."

"I got y'all."

I stopped by McDonald's for burgers and fries. When I got back, all the girls were gone and everything was cleaned up.

"Here y'all go."

"Bitch, you right on time."

They ate like they were starving.

***

We went to a big mall in Buckhead.

Jackie's salon was large. It had ten chairs in individual booths. It had ten sinks for washing hair. It had hardwood floors and ceiling fans and large windows overlooking the street.

"What's the rent here?" I asked.

"I'm not renting. I paid $100k for it."

"You must plan on making a lot of money here."

"I've gotten the booths filled. I'm asking $200 a week. In the salon, I'm asking $300."

"Well, I'm proud of you."

"Me too," Brittney and Ke'shon chimed in.

We did a big group hug.

"I'm hungry. Let's go eat," Ke'shon said.

We ate chicken and waffles at Gladys Knight Restaurant.

My phone rang. I didn't recognize the number. I let it go to voicemail.

A text came through. "BITCH YOU NOT SAFE. NEITHER IS YOUR FAMILY."

My heart raced. "I got to go to the bathroom."

"Everything good?" Jackie asked.

"Yeah."|

I washed my face as I stared in the mirror. What had I done? As tears fell, I heard a knock.

"Just a minute."

I wiped my hands and washed my face. I unlocked the bathroom and left, looking at the white woman waiting with her kids.

"You all right?" Jackie asked.

"Yeah, I just got my visitor," I lied.

"Oh."

"On top of that, Ka'wine's sick. I have to go home."

Jackie drove me to the airport.

I hated lying to my friends, but I had to know if my family was safe. I needed to tell everyone what was going on, but the time was never right.

"Call when you get back. I hope Ka'wine feels better."

"Thanks, I will."

As I waited on my plane, I called my kids' phones. There was no answer. My heart raced. I called Keith. He also didn't answer. "Shit!" I called again. It went straight to voicemail.

My legs were shaking. My nerves were shot. If anything happened to my family, I'd never forgive myself. I had put them in harm's way.

***

When my plane landed in New Orleans, I got an Uber straight to the house. It was empty.

"Ka'wine? Keith Jr.? Keith? Where are you?" I ran through the house, screaming like a crazy woman. How was I going to explain to my husband that our kids were kidnapped and it was my fault? I started to call Keith again when they all came in laughing and joking.

"Where the hell have y'all been? You need to answer the phone!" I yelled.

"Hold on, Shantell. Is everything all right?"

"I've been calling all day. I thought something had happened when nobody answered."

"I took the kids to see Pelicans and the Lakes."

"And we had fun too," the kids said, going upstairs.

"You sure you're all right?" Keith asked.

"Baby, I'm fine. I was just worried. Jet lag from the flight."

"Get some rest. I'll order a pizza. That's what the kids wanted."

"Thanks, love you."

He kissed me, and I went in the bedroom to lay down. My heart was still pounding. Thank God, my family was okay.

I had to get this straightened out before it got even more out of hand. It was stressing me the fuck out.

CHAPTER 9
Shantell

I went into Baldwin's law firm. He had called and said we needed to have an urgent discussion. As I entered, he hung up the phone.

"What's this about?" I began.

"Have a seat."

"What's going on?"

"I just got off the phone with the Feds."

"About what?"

"Deloso's prosecutor called me."

"She's been calling me too."

"They need me to convince you to testify at Deloso's trial."

"Hell no! I already told that bitch that I wasn't testifying. I have a family. Do you know what will happen if Keith finds out?" I paced back and forth over the floor.

"Do you understand the consequences if he goes free?" We in trouble."

"We? You don't have shit to do with it."

"Not according to the Feds. Deloso has a list of everyone who helped you."

"Do you hear what you're saying? I can't take the stand against this motherfucker. I had a deal. After I busted him, I didn't have to testify."

"I told them that. But since Hampton got killed, they need you."

"What the fuck am I supposed to do about Keith? If he finds out what we did, he'll kill my ass - and yours."

"He might understand."

"We're talking about Keith. He told me not to do it because this shit was going to happen. He ain't going to understand shit."

"What will you do? The trial is in a few weeks. They'll subpoena you."

"I need a cigarette."

"I didn't think you smoked."

"What? You don't think I should? My nerves are so fucking

bad, I need a line of coke."

"Shit. That bad?"

"This nigga is sending me death threats. He sent me a box with dead rats in it. If you think shit's not that bad, you're tripping."

"You need to testify. It's not just your life on the line. You got your friends and family involved too."

"I know all this shit, Baldwin."

"Think about it. Let me know something."

"I got to go. I'll let you know something."

"Please do."

I slammed his door as I walked out. I searched through my purse until I found a cigarette. With my hands shaking, I managed to light it and took a deep puff.

"Fuck! Fuck! Fuck!" I beat my hands on my steering wheel as tears streamed down my face.

***

At home, I went to a closet in my guest bedroom where I kept a couple of ounces of cocaine. I keep a stash spot because I never knew when I might need a line to settle my nervous. I'm not hooked. It makes me feel good, and it sends my sex drive through the roof. There's nothing wrong with Keith, but this shit gets me so fucking wet that it's a shame. I laid a big line on the table, rolled up a twenty, and snorted a line.

"Shit," I said, raising my head and shaking it.

I hadn't snorted any since Keith came home. I snorted a second line and my pussy got wet. I was feeling horny as shit.

I heard Keith come in. I put everything up and wiped off the table.

"Shantell! Shantell!" he yelled.

I looked in a mirror to make sure my noise was clean. When I went downstairs, he was in the kitchen with a bottle of champagne and a dozen roses.

"What's this for?" I asked, surprised.

52

"These are for you for being you." He smiled.

"But what's the occasion?"

"I got a loan to reopen my company." He popped the cork and poured champagne into two glasses.

"That's great, baby." I hugged and kissed him.

"I know. Let's go upstairs and celebrate before the kids get home. We'll go out tonight."

"I'm with that." I took his hand and led him upstairs.

***

As I bounced up and down on Keith's dick, I was thinking about what Baldwin had said. I needed to make a decision. If I didn't testify, Deloso would go free. Then he would kill my family. But he would send thugs to kill my family if I did testify. Shit, I was fucked either way.

"Yes, baby, what did you say?" I asked Keith, realizing I had missed what he said.

"You look like you're somewhere else. Like you're not interested.

"No, daddy, I'm into it."

He flipped me over, slamming his dick in and out of my pussy.

I really wasn't into it. My mind was elsewhere, but I couldn't let him know. I kept my pussy wet and hoped it wouldn't dry up before he busted his nut.

I backed up on him as he grabbed my hair and slapped me on the ass. I moaned, "Fuck yeah. Give it to me. Fuck this pussy."

As he began to shake and shoot his hot nut into my pussy, I felt like some kind of fake. My mind was on what I was going to do. Don't get it twisted: Keith always pleased me. But sex was the last thing on my mind right now.

"Damn, baby. I needed that," he said as he was catching his breath.

"It was amazing," I told him as I walked to the shower.

***

As I sat on the bed, I put on some peach Bath and Body Works lotion. I put on a black lace thong and bra from Victoria's Secret. I wore a silver and black beaded chain high-collared frock from Chanel. I got out my black Jimmy Choo "Romy" pumps that cost $600. I was wearing my mega carats diamond necklace, watch, ring, earrings, and bracelet.

Keith came out of the bathroom, drying off. He put on blue Tom Ford slacks with a white button-down shirt and blazer. He was wearing black Gucci loafers.

"How do I look?" he asked.

"Handsome."

"I'm glad we're going out."

"Me too. We need it. I'm glad you got your loan."

"I am too. I thought they would turn me down, but Baldwin worked his magic."

"I'm happy for you." I kissed him. "I'll go tell the kids we're leaving."

"I'll wait downstairs."

I went to Keith Jr.'s room. "We're going out. Call me if you need me."

"Yes, Mama."

I walked into Ka'Wine's room.

"Mama, can you please knock?"

"Sorry."

"I know you're not." She was on Facetime with someone wearing just her panties and bra.

"Are you sending pictures of yourself to boys?"

"No, Mama. I just got out of the shower. I'm talking to my friend Dana."

"We're going out. Call me if you need anything."

"Okay, have fun. And close my door."

I think this cow was sending naked pictures to some boy. We needed to have a talk. I hope she's not fucking.

Keith and I pulled off. I was happy Keith got the loan, but I knew he would. I called the bank an approved it. I left the drug game with a lot of money: $20 million offshore and $10 million in this country. The Feds didn't get it. I wasn't going to risk my life to leave empty-handed. I was smarter than that. Plus I had to cut a check to Baldwin for $1.2 million because his ass spent Keith's money. I didn't want Keith to kill him, so I was going to help out. It was the least I could do. Plus he'd been keeping his mouth closed.

Keith and I walked into the Commander's Palace. Men had to wear a jacket, and women had to be dressed up. There was a live jazz band with dance floor to the side. The bar seemed well-stocked. The tables were covered with crisp white tablecloths and topped with burning candles.

"Can I take your order?" the slim white waitress asked.

"Bring us some white wine. We'll both get lobster and shrimps," Keith said.

"Be back in a minute with your drinks."

"It's really nice in here, baby," I said.

"It is. I've never been here. They opened after I went to prison."

"Yeah."

"Here's your wine. The meat will be out soon." The waitress placed glasses in front us.

Keith proposed a toast. "To a new beginning."

"For sure."

We sat and ate and talked about how our life would be different when we moved to Atlanta.

"Come on, baby, let's dance. They're playing our song," Keith said.

It was Freddie Jackson's "You Are My Lady". I never wanted this night to end. The way Keith was holding me made me melt. I was turned on.

Later, I stood at the bar, sipping on a drink. Keith was in the restroom.

I heard a voice beside me. "Hey, pretty lady. You can't call nobody no more?"

"Darrell? What are you doing here?"

"I'm in New Orleans on business. I was hoping I would see you."

I looked him up and down. He was dressed in an all-white linen outfit. His hair was cut low and waves banging with his beard well-trimmed. He was looking good, I'm not going to lie.

"I'm here with my husband."

"I saw you with the tall handsome guy."

"How long you been here?"

"Long enough to see you slow dance with him."

"You stalking me?"

"No. I come here all the time when I come to New Orleans. So what's up with us?"

"I told you, we're done. You knew my husband got out of jail."

"I know you did. But I couldn't get you out of my head and heart. Did you tell him about us?"

"What? No. Why would I do that? It's not his business. We're through."

"If you don't want him to find out, meet me at the Hilton on Canal Street. Room 722. Or else your husband's going to know his wife wasn't good while he was in prison."

"You're blackmailing me?"

"Call it what you want. Just show up." He walked away.

"Who was that you were talking to?" Keith asked.

"Some guy trying to flirt with me. I told him I was married, and he left me alone. You know how men are when they see a pretty woman in a club by herself."

"For a minute, I thought you knew him."

"No. Why would you think I knew him?"

"The way he looked at me when I came up. It was like y'all had something going on."

"No. Let's get out of here. We can go home and make love."

"I'm with that." Keith kissed me.

***

Darrell

As I watched Shantell leave the club with her husband, I'm not going to lie, I was jealous. Seeing her again brought back all my old feelings.

When her ass came to the hotel tomorrow I was going to put that dick on her like never before and make her leave that nigga again. This time I was going to put a baby in her ass. I was still in love with her.

Just then my phone rang and interrupted my thoughts. I looked down at it. It was a call from Mexico. I didn't feel like dealing with that shit right now.

***

Shantell

As Keith was going down on me, I was thinking about Darrell. I remembered how he ate my pussy and licked my asshole. He had me climbing the walls.

I grabbed Keith's head hard, grinding my pussy in his face.

"Fuck yeah, baby. Eat this pussy." I had to be careful not to call him Darrell.

Keith slid his dick into me as I dug my nails into his back.

I knew I was wrong for thinking of another man as I was getting dick from my husband, but I couldn't help it. I was shaking as he shot his nut into me.

I laid on his chest, sweaty and thinking about another man, as he played with my hair.

Robert Baptiste

CHAPTER 10
Shantell

As I got off the elevator at the hotel, a thousand thoughts were running through my mind. I shouldn't be here. If Keith found out I was visiting another man in his hotel room, he wouldn't be trying to hear shit from me. He would fuck me and this nigga up. But I couldn't have this nigga telling Keith shit. I had to figure out a way to keep this nigga's mouth closed until I could figure something out.

As I walked down the hall, I had second and third thoughts. I was playing with fire. I still had feelings for Darrell. They didn't just go away like that. I'd seen him for a couple of years. At one time I was willing to leave my husband in prison and go off with him. If not for our kids, Keith would still be in prison and Darrell and I would be married.

I got to room 722 and nervously knocked. There was no answer. I exhaled a sigh of relief and walked away from the door as he opened it behind me.

"Shantell."

I turned around and walked back to his room. He wasn't wearing a shirt. His six pack was showing, and his chest was puffed up like he'd been doing push-ups. He was wearing some gray boxer briefs.

"Come in. I thought you might stand me up."

I'm not going to lie. My panties were soaking wet. Lord help me. I knew I shouldn't have come. This nigga still turned me on.

"What do you want, Darrell?"

"You."

"You can't have me."

"Why not?"

"You know why. I'm married."

"So why did you come?"

"You said you would tell. You were blackmailing me."

"I wouldn't do it. You know I love you."

"I hear you."

Robert Baptiste

"Looks like you gained some weight."
"That's from all the good living with Keith."
"Like we used to do." He kissed me.
I broke away. "Stop."
"Do you really want me to?"
He tongue kissed me. I kissed him back.

He led me to the bed and took off my panties and jeans simultaneously. I grabbed his head with my legs shaking. I came in his mouth. I knew it was wrong, but it felt so good.

He climbed on top of me, easing his hard ten inch dick into my wet pussy. He put my legs on his shoulders, thrusting harder and deeper into my pussy walls.

I was losing control. "I'm cumming. Please don't stop."
"Do you love me?"
"Y-Y-Yes," I stuttered.

He thrust even deeper as I came back to back. He flipped me onto my stomach and thrust his dick in and out of my pussy as he lay on top of me. He kissed and sucked on my neck. It felt so good, I came hard again. I gripped his hand as he shot his hot cum into me.

"Fuck. I love you." He was playing with my hair.
"Look. We can't be together."
"Why not? I love you, and you love me."
"I'm in love with my husband."
"I don't care."
"But I do."
"Look, if I can have a piece of your heart, I'll be good."
"My husband's back."
He kissed me. I wanted to tell him to stop, but it felt so good.
"You making this too hard."

As I left the hotel, my feelings were all over the place.

I'm a real dumb bitch. I got a good family and things are going good. Right now, though, I'm in a hotel fucking another man who can ruin everything.

I hoped fucking him was enough that he wouldn't tell Keith.

60

***

When I got home, I hoped Keith didn't want to fuck. My pussy was already sore.

Keith was working on his laptop.

"Hey, baby," I said as I kissed him.

"Where've you been?"

"Working at the salon. I had to make sure my books were ready for taxes."

"I've been trying to call you all day."

"I'm sorry I missed your calls. I was so busy. I'm going to take a shower."

"I'll be up shortly. I'm working on a plan for my company."

I got in the shower and let the hot water run over my body. I was thinking about Darrell. I'm not going to lie. All my feelings for him had come back. But I loved my husband too. I think Darrell will keep his mouth shut as long as I fuck him.

When I got back to the bedroom, Keith was already asleep. Thank God. My pussy couldn't take no more beating. That nigga Darrell already had me walking funny.

I got in bed and instantly fell asleep.

Robert Baptiste

CHAPTER 11
Shantell
Three weeks later

I jumped out of bed and ran to the bathroom to throw up.

"Shit! My stomach's hurting."

I leaned back over the toilet and threw up again. As I flushed the toilet, I thought about what I had eaten. I rinsed out my mouth and brushed my teeth. I looked in the mirror. I looked stressed the fuck out. Calls from the prosecutor and Baldwin. The anonymous calls. The daily news coverage.

I needed to see a doctor. I had the same symptoms I had when I was pregnant with Ka'wine. There was a strong possibility that my ass was pregnant from all the fucking Keith and I had been doing lately.

The next morning, I took a hot shower. I put on tight black DKNY jeans with a matching shirt and sandals.

At the doctor's office, I signed in at the receptionist desk.

"I'm here to see Dr. McCann for my six month checkup."

"I'll let her know you're here."

"Thanks."

I sat in the chair, looking at my Facebook page to see who had hit me up. As I was responding to my messages, the doctor called my name. I followed her into the examination room. She was an older white lady with long blonde hair. She'd been my doctor since Keith Jr. was born.

The nurse took my blood pressure. I hope I didn't blow the machine up. I figured it was off the chart.

The doctor rolled next to me. "So what brings you in today?"

"My six month check, and I think I may be pregnant."

"Morning sickness?"

"I've been throwing up."

"Take off your clothes and lay back on the table. Let's check you out. The nurse is going to draw some blood." She pressed on my stomach. "Does it hurt?" She checked my vagina. "Everything's good down there."

"Good."

The nurse took some blood. Thirty minutes later, the doctor returned, smiling. "I have wonderful news. You're pregnant. Congratulations."

"Thank you." I shook her hand as I got up.

"Come back in two weeks for your first follow-up."

"Will do."

I got in my G truck, smiling from ear to ear. I couldn't wait to get home and tell Keith. He wanted another boy.

Then it hit me. This could be Darrell's baby too. We were fucking around the same time.

Shit! I must be the dumbest bitch in the world.

CHAPTER 12
Shantell

I couldn't believe I was pregnant, and maybe by another man. I sat on the couch, rubbing my stomach. How could I explain this to husband? How could I come to Keith without him beating the fuck out of me? Could I even manage to tell him I might be pregnant by another man from another state? This nigga was going to kill my ass. The only thing he asked was that I not get pregnant while he was in prison. I actually did, but an abortion took care of that. My dumb black ass waited until he got home and then fucked another man, who was my lover while he was in prison. I didn't think my life could get any worse.

Shit, I didn't even talk to Darrell anymore. When he called, I sent his ass straight to voice mail. I don't need Keith to find out about me and him. I called myself fucking him so Keith didn't find out, but now look.

I guess I should confess to Keith. If he ever found out, it was going to be hell to tell the captain.

I'd changed my number three times, but Darrell kept finding me. I was never going to tell him that he may be the father of the baby I'm carrying. Hell no! Both of them niggas would be at war trying to kill themselves over me. I couldn't forgive myself if either one got hurt over me.

When I was around Darrell, it was magic. I can't explain it. My pussy calls for his dick when he's around. It feels like it knows when I'm around him.

But I love my husband. I swear I do.

My phone rang. It was my mother. I answered, "Hey, Mom."

"When are we going out for a little girl time? I need my nails done and a trip to the spa."

"Okay, I'll meet you there."

I thought about telling my mother, but she has a big fucking mouth and is against abortion.

When it fucking rains, it fucking pours.

***

"Oh, yeah, this shit feels good." I was lying on a table getting a massage.

"Yes, it's good," my mother said. "How is everything?"

"It's all good."

"You and Keith been fucking like rabbits? Huh?"

"Mom!"

"Girl, it ain't no secret. He was gone a long time. I'm surprised you've not already pregnant. It looks like you're gaining weight."

"For real?"

"Yes. All in your face."

"I'm not. It's just been all the lovemaking and all the food I've cooked for him."

"I've been getting some myself."

"Mom! Too much information."

"I'm not over the hill. I still like to get my freak on."

"Spare me."

"What's Keith been doing?"

"He's trying to open a new construction company."

"I hope he do it right this time."

"He did it right the first time. His friend got fucked up and told on him."

"He needs to find better friends. How are my grandkids?"

"They're fine. They love that their daddy's home."

"I see. They barely come by to see me."

"They're teenagers now. They don't even have time for me. Ka'wine is into boys, and Keith Jr. is into girls and video games."

"They are around that age. Time moves so fast, I swear. It seems like just yesterday I was taking them out for ice cream."

"Come on, let's get out of here. I'm hungry."

"Okay, but you need to go to the doctor and get checked out."

"Mom, I'm fine."

"You never know."

"Whatever."

I hope she was playing. I didn't need Keith getting all excited about a baby that might not be his. I was probably not going to keep it. As I looked in the rearview mirror, I noticed my face did look fat.

***

I woke up at 3:00 a.m. My stomach was killing me. As I began to piss, it felt like there was a lot of water coming out of me. I touched my pussy. When I pulled back, my hand, I saw blood. I knew it meant I was having a miscarriage. I had a couple before Keith Jr. was born.

I started to cry. I had thought about an abortion, but I really wanted to keep this baby. I knew this was happening because of all the low down shit I was doing. I was married and doing fucked-up shit on my husband.

I needed to get my shit together.

Robert Baptiste

CHAPTER 13
Shantell

I was sitting on the doctor's table. I needed to be sure I had been right.

"So what's going on?" I asked.

"I'm sorry. You had a miscarriage."

I had known it, but verification still hurt.

"How are you feeling?"

"My body feels fine, but my heart is hurting."

"I'm truly sorry."

I started getting dressed, "Thank you, Doctor."

"You will need to come back for a follow-up, or if you feel worse."

"I will."

"I'm going to prescribe something to help you with pain."

I got back in my car mad as a motherfucker. Tears were flooding down my face. I needed to talk to someone. It felt as if I was having a nervous breakdown.

Baldwin called, but I couldn't deal with him. I couldn't be bothered with that bullshit today.

I was in some deep shit. The more I tried to get out, the deeper I got. Dealing with that motherfucker Deloso had a bitch stressed the fuck out. This motherfucker got a really long arm. If he wanted me dead, he could reach me from behinds bars.

To show what a piece of shit I am, I hadn't even told my friends that their lives were in danger.

I pulled off the road and called an old friend, Taraji, but the phone went to voicemail. I cursed and drove on.

Eventually, I found myself at a church in a confessional. Nobody was there but me and God.

"God, I know I ain't been doing right by you. If you help me out of this situation, I promise I will go to church every Sunday and stop messing with women, cheating on my husband, and even doing drugs.

The door slid back, scaring the shit out of me.

"How long has it been since your last confession?"

"It's been a long time."

"What's on your mind, my child?"

"Well, Father…" I wanted to tell him, but I just couldn't.

"It okay, child. God will forgive all sins."

"Father, I've got to go. Ask God to forgive me."

I fled the booth and the church.

I soon ended up at Taraji's house. Her car was out front. Taraji was one of my best friends from my project days. We used to jump bitches at school together. She was a hood rat, just like Kesha had been.

The bitch got lucky and married an NBA player. That shit didn't last long. She had his baby. She settled for $10 million in the divorce, and the nigga still paid her child support. She had a big house in Slidell. All she did was fuck big baller niggas who were in the drug game and who played some kind of sport. I'm not mad at her.

I walked to her door. It had been a minute since I talked to or saw her. I talked to her a couple times since I saw her in the club in Atlanta, but that had been like over three years ago.

I felt I could talk to her. Because she was not involved, she could give me some good advice. Moreover, the bitch was not judgmental. The bitch gives it to you raw and uncut. She shoots from the hip and doesn't hold back her punches.

I knocked. I hoped she was at home. She was always trying to get niggas to fly her out of town.

"Who is it?" she asked through the door.

"Me. Shantell." *Thank you, Jesus*, I thought.

She opened the door. She was smoking a blunt. She was wearing gray boy shorts and a pink wifebeater. Her hair was short and dyed gold. She wasn't wearing shoes and her fingernails and toes were painted the same color as her hair. She looked like LaLa Anthony. She had a big fake ass. We had hooked up a few times back in the game. The bitch got some good pussy.

"Hey, baby," she said as she grabbed me tight and jumped up and down with me.

I took the blunt from her mouth and walked into the living room. I paced back and forth as I hit the blunt.

"What's going on?"

"I need something strong to drink."

"I got some Patron."

"Good. We'll need the whole bottle." "

"Bitch, this must be serious. I'll be right back. Take your damn shoes off. You're walking on my white carpet."

"My bad."

She came back with two shot glasses and a bottle of Patron and sat down across from me. I poured Patron in a shot glass and gulped it down. She took one with me.

"Shit," I said, standing back up and pacing again.

"Tell me what's going on? It must be life and death from the way you pacing."

I didn't know if I wanted to sit or keep pacing. I hit the blunt again, blowing the smoke out my nose.

"Damn, bitch, it must be serious. Sit down and tell me what's on your mind before you go crazy."

"Bitch, I'm about to have a nervous breakdown."

"Over what?"

"Taraji, I need you to promise not to say anything to anyone. I mean nobody. This shit can get you killed, I'm telling you."

"Bitch, you know we got secrets. I've never told anybody anything about when you cheated on Keith and had an abortion. I never told nobody.

"But this bigger than that. That's small change."

"I got you. I promise not to tell anyone. Have you killed somebody?"

I didn't say shit. Her eyes looked as if they were going to burst from her face. She had a serious look on her face.

I took a deep breath and hit the Patron straight from the bottle.

"Do you need to get out of town?" she asked.

"No."

"Do you need money?"

"No."

"Who was it?"

"Look, here's the business. My life is fucked up. I think I'm going to die. My family too. It's all my fault." A tear rolled down my face.

"What do you mean? Don't say that."

"I did something Keith told me not to do."

"What?"

"See, Keith went to prison for thirty years for drugs and murder."

"What?"

"Yeah, one of his bitch-ass friends told on him. This nigga named Dave."

"I thought Keith was out of the game?"

"He was. But the nigga brought up some murder that Keith did. To keep himself out of prison."

"That's some bitch-ass shit. That nigga need a killing. Old bitch-ass nigga."

"They killed him. And his family."

"That's good."

"Well, now they want to kill me."

"What? Why?"

"The Feds wanted Keith to tell on his cartel connect, but he wouldn't. I went undercover for them. I set up the head of the cartel so Keith could get out of prison. Now if I don't testify against him, he'll go free and kill my whole family."

She started laughing. "Bitch, you need to leave the drugs alone. I've heard it all. You working for Feds to bust a cartel leader. Bitch, stop playing."

"Do you see me smiling? Bitch, I'm dead serious." I jumped up from the couch.

"Bitch, you dead serious?"

"Like your daddy when he caught that heart attack."

"Fuck, what are you going to do?"

"I don't know."

"Bitch, what did you do? They don't play. They're going to kill you."

"You think?"

"Have you told Keith?"

"Fuck no! The only people that know is me, my lawyer, and the Feds. And now you."

"You're in some serious shit. You need me to help you get out of the country?

"That won't help."

"Will you tell Keith?"

"I don't know. But it's not just him. There's also a few others who don't know their life is in danger."

"You're going to leave them in the dark? You're a piece of shit if you do that. They might think Keith put you up to it."

"I know that. And that's not true."

"Bitch, you need to go to the Feds and tell them everything. They can protect you and your family."

"But Keith will find out."

"Better he find out and leave you then you ending up in a box."

"I know." I lay my head on her lap and cried as she rubbed my back.

"Damn, you in some tough shit. You have to testify against this motherfucker and try to get your family into witness protection. That way, you know your family's safe and he's in prison."

"I'll think about it."

"It'll be all right. I'm telling you."

"I don't know about all that."

"Fuck all that. I haven't seen you in four years. Tonight, we're going to go out and party. If it's your last day on earth, you might as well live. Besides, I haven't been out in years."

"You?"

"I'm slowing down these days. I got a daughter to think about."

"How old is she now?"

"Five."

"Where's her bad ass at?"

"With her grandmother, who spoils her rotten. While I got this free time, we will hit up a few clubs in the city. You know how we do."

"I got you."

"I love you." She hugged and kissed me.

***

I put on my snakeskin Atelier Versace outfit with my black Bare and Bodacious sandals. I put on some red lipstick. I brushed out my hair, letting it hang down my back. I put on a diamond necklace and watch. I put on Tiffany's perfume, grabbed a white Versace purse, and headed downstairs.

Keith was working on his laptop.

"Baby, I'm going out." I kissed him.

"Have fun."

"I will."

I got in my white G wagon. I took a deep breath to clear my head of the bullshit that was going on. I hadn't gotten any calls or dead rats in a while.

Maybe it was not as bad as I thought. Maybe Deloso just wanted to get my attention so I wouldn't tell on him. I decided I couldn't live in fear. I had to live my life. I was going out to get lit.

I rang Taraji's door bell.

"Come in."

"Bitch, you not ready yet?"

"I'm trying to find something to wear."

"Bitch, you got a closet full of shit. Just pick something and let's bounce."

"Bitch, I know you're not talking. Not with the way you take forever to get dressed."

"Whatever."

She put on a black leather Isabel Maront skirt and matching top. She was wearing black wrapped ankle mini-heels. "How do I look?"

"Pretty."

She added fake eyelashes and blue lipstick.

"We're taking my truck tonight. I don't want to get blown

up."

"You got jokes?"

"I'm just playing."

We got in her blue Range Rover. It had big chrome rims and blue-tinted windows.

We drove over to a club called the Metro. There was a line around the corner. It was always packed on Thursday. We went to the VIP line. I tipped the bouncer a hundred and went in.

It was packed from wall to wall with fine-ass niggas and hoes. The DJ was blasting Drake through the speakers.

"Bitch, I see it hasn't changed much since I've been out," Taraji said.

"How long has it been?"

"Almost three years."

"It's been a year for me."

"The only thing I see that's changed is the hoes and niggas are finer."

"You ain't lying." We dapped each other off.

"Let's go to the VIP."

"Okay."

We chilled in the VIP section drinking strawberry Ciroc and shots of Patron.

"Here, bitch, pop this." She handed me pills.

"What's this?"

"A molly. It'll have you turned up."

After I took it, we were on the dance floor a couple of minutes later. We twerked our asses on niggas and bitches and each other. My pussy was soaking wet, and I was horny as hell.

We hit a new strip club called the Spade that was near the Superdome. There were a bunch of fine-ass, butt-naked females of all colors and nationalities

We got four thousand in ones and some Ciroc at the bar. We sat at the table and watched as a fine black bitch twerked to a Drake song.

A couple of redbones walked over to us. "Y'all want a lap dance?"

"Sure, why not?" I said.

They were both thick as government cheese. They had long black wavy hair that hung down to their big fake tattooed asses. They looked like a mix of black and Creole.

I grabbed the girl's ass as it was bouncing up and down on me. She took me to a private room for a lap dance. I rubbed all over her ass as she put a show on for me.

Full of mollies and liquored out of my mind, Taraji and I finally left the club alone. I passed out at her house.

CHAPTER 14
Keith

I pulled up at my sister's house in Kenner. I hadn't seen her since I got home.

When we were growing up in the projects, I took care of her and my mother. Once I got on, I moved them out of the Calliope Projects to a big house in the eastern part of New Orleans. My mother died five years later, so I just kept taking care of my sister. We have different fathers. My father was killed and her father went to jail right after she was born.

Before I went to jail, I made sure she was straight. I put a million dollars in a bank account for her and my little nephew. Not that she needed it. She's an RN who married a doctor who treats her like a queen.

I didn't call her to say I was coming. I doubt she even knew I was out. I figured she'd cuss me out for not coming sooner.

As I pulled up, I knew she was there because her blue G wagon was parked out front. She stayed in the affluent part of Kenner. Houses started at a quarter million. She's doing good for herself. She'd been a nurse ever since she came home from the Army. I'm proud of her.

I knocked on the door.

"Who is it?" she asked. Then I heard her scream.

I saw her looking through the peephole. The door flew open. She jumped in my arms and hugged me tight. She had come often to see me in Beaumont except when we were on lockdown. She made me call her so she would know I was good. She would do anything I needed her to. I trusted her with my life. She had helped me with my first construction company, handling the paperwork and all. She had been my company's president.

"What? How?" She seemed stunned.

"I won my appeal."

"How long have you been out?"

"Almost a month."

"And your ass is just now coming to see me?"

"I had to put things together."

"Yeah, sure. You've been too busy digging in Shantell's ass. Get in here."

"Yes, Mother."

She was the youngest child, but acted like the oldest. She acted and looked just like my mother. In fact, they could have been twins. She was short, thick, and yellow-skinned. She had long wavy black hair and big dimples. She is Creole and black mixed.

"I'm glad you caught me. I'm on my lunch break."

"Where is Chris?"

"At school. Here's some pictures of him at a football game."

"He's playing football now?"

"Wide receiver."

"Is he good?"

"Number one in the nation. The college coaches keep calling and asking where he's going to go to college.

"The boy is tall."

"6'1." Same as your ass. Where are those kids of yours?"

"In school. They're both doing well. Ka'wine is into that damn boy shit. Keith Jr. is into software and girls."

"That's good. Bring them to see me."

"Shantell didn't bring them over?"

"She did at first, but she stopped a couple of years ago."

"I'll make sure I bring them by."

"I'll hold you to that. What are you going to do now?"

"I'm reopening my construction company."

"Do you need the money you gave me? I still have it."

"Nah. I got a loan from the bank."

"Where are you going to put it this time?"

"Here in Kenner. That why I'm out here, to look for a spot."

"So that's why your ass came over?"

"Nah, you know I love you." I hugged her.

"I love you too, but I got to get back to work."

"I thought you was about to retire?

"Some of us have to work for a. living. We have bills."

"You got a million in the bank. You can start your own business."

"That's for rainy days."

"Where's your husband?"

"You mean my ex-husband?"

"What?"

"His ass got some young bitch pregnant. I guess my pussy got too old."

"How long has this been going on?"

"About a year and a half. The divorce will be final in a few weeks. He already has a new house and everything."

"Sorry to hear it. If you need anything, I'm here."

"My new boyfriend is here too."

"Boyfriend?"

"What? You thought I'd let this fine body go to waste?"

"Whatever."

"I got to get back to work."

"Okay. Love you." We hugged.

As I drove away, my phone rang. Someone on the other end just breathed without talking. When I hung up, they sent me a picture of a rat eating cheese. Someone

must have sent it to the wrong number. I deleted it.

I texted my wife and Baldwin to meet me in Kenner at my new office.

***

Shantell

A text woke me up. It was from Baldwin. In all CAPS, he said we needed to talk and that I needed to meet him at three at the federal courthouse.

I grabbed my clothes as I looked over at Taraji. I smiled as I thought of our crazy night and the wild time we had with the strippers.

I got dressed and left. I sent Taraji a message, and then sent one to Keith. I had told him I was spending the night at Taraji's house because I was too drunk to drive.

At home, I took some Advil. Upstairs, I fell asleep in a hot bubble bath. Two texts awoke me.

The first was from Taraji. She told me how much fun she had, and that she wanted to do it again. She also asked when I could go shopping. I told her Saturday.

The other message was from Baldwin. He said I needed to get to the courthouse.

I didn't want to be bothered by this shit anymore. At this point, what would happen would happen. But I had to worry about my family. I quickly got dressed in blue skinny jeans, red top, and tan red bottoms. I grabbed my purse to head for the courthouse.

At the court building, my stomach started hurting. I hated coming to this motherfucker on Camp Street. Nothing good came from here. You're either ratting, or you're getting a lot of time. Then you wish you would have told on someone.

I entered the building after climbing the large white steps. Federal agents were everywhere. I put my ring in the basket and walked through the scanner. I took the elevator to the fifth floor.

I shouldn't even be here. I needed to turn my ass around, leave this motherfucker, and go home. They could figure this shit out.

My stomach was in knots as I walked down the hallway. I sent Baldwin a text that I was here, and he came out to greet me.

"I'm glad you made it."

"I started not to come. They don't need me. They have more than enough evidence on him. Plus they have him killing a federal agent."

"Come on. They're waiting for us."

"They?"

"The prosecutor and a couple of FBI agents."

I looked at him like he was crazy. "They get to talking that bullshit, I'm out. Just to let you know ahead of time."

"Okay."

In the conference room, a slim black woman wearing a blue Prada dress stood up. Beside her, there were two FBI agents.

"Ms. Washington, I'm glad you made it. I'm prosecuting this case now. The last prosecutor is no longer with us." I stared at her. "My name is Sandra Lewis. I know about your situation with both the cartel and your husband. I think we can help you."

"I don't mean to interrupt, but I don't see why you need me at all."

"I'll tell you."

"Tell me what?"

"First, we need you to think about witness protection."

"That's out."

"You shouldn't rule it out."

"It's not going to happen. Period."

"You're dealing with powerful people."

"Ain't he locked up?"

"Yes."

"So why are you wasting my time."

"We need a favor."

"From me? The last time I got in bed with you, shit went sideways."

"I promise it won't be like that. This time, I'm in charge."

"This shit always seems the same to me."

"We really need you."

"I don't have time for this bullshit. I've got a business to run." I stood up.

"I'll explain everything. Please sit."

"I'm listening."

She looked at me, then Baldwin.

"Baldwin, what's going on?"

"She's going to tell you. Now."

"As you know, Eric Hampton was killed in jail. Deloso put a hit out on him."

"What does that have to do with me? I fulfilled my part. I brought him down. You promised I wouldn't have to testify."

"You're right. But our key witness is dead."

"You've got him red-handed for killing a DEA agent. What else do you need?"

"With a cartel boss, you need more. You need a member of the inner circle to take the stand."

"I'm not going to get on the stand and point that motherfucker out."

"Then your life will be in danger."

"Tell me something I don't know."

"Picture what will happen to your family if he walks."

"Can't I just write something?"

"We need you there. You have to tell the jury about him."

"I don't know. This shit is open to the public. When my husband finds out I'm taking the stand, do you know what he's going to do? He'll kill my ass. Especially since he told my dumb ass not to do it in the first place."

"He'll never know. We can close the trial to the public and seal the record. We can protect you if you need it."

"What can you do if this nigga tries to blow up my house or car?"

"We can put you and your family in Witness Protection."

"What about my friends?"

"We can help them as well."

"No thanks. They don't know."

"You need to tell them. Trial date is in two weeks."

"I'll let you know something in a couple of days."

"Please do. Remember, we can subpoena you. Your husband will surely know when a marshal comes to get you."

"I won't say anything. I'll plead the Fifth."

"Then your husband will return to jail."

"I'll tell the newspapers how the government defrauds people by blackmailing them. The *New York Times* and CNN will have a field day with that. A wife cuts and fulfills a deal to get her husband out of prison, but they send him back to jail because his wife is afraid."

"We'll see."

"Try me, bitch!"

"Enough," Baldwin interrupted. "Let's go, Shantell."

I stormed out of the office. Baldwin caught me at the

elevators. "What was that shit about?" he grumbled.

"I could ask you the same thing. You let me walk right into a trap."

"That's the reality of this. They don't have to play fair. If you cut a deal with the devil, you got to pay whatever he wants."

"But they owe me."

"Sure, but what good does it do?"

As we left, we got a text from Keith.

I followed Baldwin to Kenner. Keith was outside on a big open lot. There was a rundown building with a lot of old construction equipment laying around.

"Hey, baby." I hugged and kissed him.

"Were y'all together?" he asked.

"No, we just got here at the same time," I said.

"Why are we here? Baldwin asked.

"I wanted to show my two best people my new construction company."

"How much did you pay?" Baldwin asked.

"They wanted $1.2 million, but I talked them down to a million. What do you think, baby?"

"I'll take a lot of work to make it work."

"I know. I'll put all my time in it."

"I'm proud of you, baby."

"Me too, man," added Baldwin.

"Now, I'm going to need y'all to invest with me!"

"Baby, you know I'm in."

We walked through the gate and looked at the old building and equipment.

"Baby, you sure about this?"

"I can make it work."

"You could get something in better shape," Baldwin said.

"Yeah, but one guy was selling for five million and he still wanted a percentage."

"You should have jumped on that," Baldwin said.

"I don't have five million. I'm not in the drug game no more. They took all of my money." Keith's phone rang. "Whoever this dumb motherfucker is who's playing on my phone, I'm going to fuck them up once I find out who it is."

"What's going on?"

"Someone keeps sending me pictures of a rat eating cheese. See?"

"Just delete it. Don't let that shit wreck your nerves. They probably sent it to the wrong person. That shit happens all the time.

"Sure does," Baldwin said, looking at me.

"Y'all are right. I'm tripping."

"Look, bro. I've got to get back to the office." Baldwin dapped him off.

"Later."

"Baby, I have to get home and fix some food. It's getting late."

"I'm right behind you."

I pulled away angry. Now they were sending shit to Keith. Ain't this a bitch?

I needed to send this nigga away for life, before Keith found out what was going on. They might think he put me up to it. The truth is, he didn't have nothing to do with this bullshit. It was all on me.

FUCK!

CHAPTER 15
Shantell

Taraji and I were walking through the mall shopping for clothes and shoes. We were going out this weekend. Also, I needed to tell her what the prosecutor said and about the messages that Keith was receiving on his phone.

"How's shit coming with the case? You said you went and talked to the prosecutor."

"Bitch, that hoe is talking about subpoenaing me to come to court and they will send the U.S. Marshalls to come get me if I don t show up.

"Can she do that?"

"According to Baldwin, she can."

"What? Them bitches are playing dirty."

"That's not all. The bitch told me that if I don't testify, she would send Keith back to prison."

"Damn, that bitch is raw."

"Those bitches don't play fair. I wish I had never gotten involved in this shit. This not panning out like I thought it would. It just fucked my life up even worse. I should have kept Keith's ass in prison and kept fucking Darrell."

"Damn, bitch, that's how you feel? Who is Darrell?"

"Damn, I said his name out loud?"

"Yes, bitch, who is this mystery man?"

"He was a man I was dealing with when Keith was in prison."

"How does he look?"

I knew I was down bad for having his pictures in my phone. But he hit me up a couple of days ago. He sent me a dick pic and a shot of him naked. I should have deleted them, but he is so fine. I got wet just thinking about him.

"Damn. His ass is fine."

"Here's his dick."

"Bitch, his shit is big. I see why you don't want to let him go. He got a brother?"

"Not that I know of."

"So what is your married ass doing with a naked man and a big dick in your phone?"

"Let's go get something to eat. It's a long story."

We grabbed some fried chicken and fries and sat at a table.

I started, "When Keith went to prison, I met Darrell. He's sweet, charming, and fun to be around. The sex was great. We fell in love. I was going to marry him, but I changed my mind when I took the kids to visit Keith. I had fallen out of love with Keith, but I still have love for him. And the kids need him."

"Let me get this right. You fell in love with Darrell, but kept your feelings inside. You dealing with Keith so he can be with the kids. Do you still love Keith?"

"Yes."

"But you're not in love with him?"

"That's where shit's fucked up."

"It's not hard. Either you in love with him, or you're not."

"I just lost a baby."

"Whose baby?"

I took a deep breath.

"Oh hell no. Darrell?" she asked.

"I think so. We had sex around that time."

"Bitch, I thought I was a hoe."

"He's asked me to come to Houston for a few days."

"Does he know about the baby?"

"No."

"Are you going to see him?"

"I don't know. I'm only fucking him because I don't want him to tell Keith about me and him."

"Do you like being in love with him?"

"I don't know. I need to end this shit. Keith doesn't need to find out. He won't take this shit lightly. He'll kill us both."

"Bitch, you have a lot of drama going your way. I see why you're having a nervous breakdown." '

"Bitch, it gets worse."

"How?"

"Somebody is sending Keith pictures of a rat eating cheese."

"What? I thought he didn't know anything about it."

"He doesn't."

"Bitch, this is getting serious."

"You think?"

"You need to get in the witness protection."

"I don't know about all that."

"So what are you going to do?"

Tears came to my eyes. "I don't know yet."

She pulled me to her. "I got your back. No matter what, I love you and I'm here for you."

"Thanks." I wiped away my tears.

"Now, let's finish shopping."

***

Later, we want to a Nikki Minaj concert. Afterwards, we want to a strip club called SHE SHE. It was holding an after party. It was off the chain with butt-naked bitches everywhere.

I was high on molly that Taraji gave me and I had drunk a couple of bottles of Ciroc. I'm not going to lie; I needed this. I was fucking stressed out. I didn't have a clue what I was going to do about the trial shit or Darrell. But I needed to do something.

Two black bitches walked over to us. "Y'all want a couple of lap dances?"

"Sure."

They started shaking their asses on us. I grabbed one to bounce her up and down on me.

We stayed a while longer, then left the strip club with a couple of hoes.

At Taraji's house, I ground my pussy into the redbone's face as I came back to back.

"Yeah, yeah, eat this pussy," I moaned. Lord, I needed this.

I looked over. Taraji was eating the other stripper out. Ultimately, we all had one huge orgasm. There were no sounds but moaning and pussy-licking all night.

The next morning, I woke up with a headache. I was still high from the previous night. Unfortunately, all the freaking and getting high didn't get everything off my mind.

I put on my clothes and left. As I got in the car, I got a text from Baldwin asking what I was going to do.

I didn't even text him back.

CHAPTER 16
Shantell

When I got home, everyone was gone. I slept about four hours and then took a bath.

I went downstairs to cook dinner. We hadn't eaten as a family in months. The kids were teens and had their own things going on. Keith was trying to start a new business. I had too much going on.

As I started water to boil, Keith called.

"Hey, baby," I answered.

"Hey, what's up?"

"I'm starting dinner. Will you be home early?"

"It'll be later on. I'm trying to get a contract with the city."

"I know. But we haven't been spending any time together."

"I promise I'll make it up to you. Love you."

"Love you too."

Next, Ka'wine called me. "Mama, I'm staying at Katrina's house tonight."

"But I'm making dinner."

"I know. But I'll eat here. We have a lot of studying to do."

Finally, Keith Jr. called. "Mama, I'm staying with Chris. His daddy is taking us to laser tag."

"Be safe. Call when you get back to his house."

"I will."

"Well, so much for dinner."

Then my phone rang again. I thought one of them had changed their mind.

"Hey, beautiful, I haven't heard from you in a minute." It was Darrell.

My pussy instantly got wet. I swear I wanted to leave his ass alone, but I couldn't. That's why my ass was in this situation in the first place, from all the bullshit I'd been doing. "You know I've been busy."

"I'm in your city for a minute. I'd love to see you."

"I don't know about that."

"It's not like you're doing shit."

"Well…"

"Well, what?"

"Okay."

I got into a pink Chanel dress, no panties, and my pink Chanel heels. I decided if Keith didn't want to spend time with me, I'd spend time with someone else.

Darrell told me to meet him in Houston's, a restaurant in Slidell. When I entered, he waved me over to the table.

This man gets finer and finer.

I still hadn't told him about the miscarriage, and I didn't plan to. I needed to break this off. I couldn't keep doing this to my husband.

"Hey." I got to his table, smiling.

"You look good," he said.

"Thanks,"

"Can I get a hug?" he asked.

I hugged him. Lord, this man smelled good. My pussy got soaked. He pulled out my chair.

"Thank you."

"No problem."

"So how's everything?"

"It's all good. Why haven't you called?"

"Look, Darrell, we need to talk."

"About?"

"Us."

"Come on, let's go outside and talk."

It was a little cold outside, so we got into his black Rover. And before I knew it, I was riding his dick in the parking lot. Good thing he had tinted windows.

"Yes, I'm cumming!" I said, bouncing up and down on his dick.

"Me too."

He shot his nut all in me as I came all over his dick. I got off the seat, trying to catch my breath.

"Now what you want to talk about?" he asked.

"I can't keep doing this?"

"Doing what?"

"Us."

"I thought there wasn't an us."

"There's not."

"So what's wrong?" he asked.

"Us fucking each other. That's what's wrong."

"I didn't realize it was a problem."

"Look, your sex is good. It's great. Lord knows I want to fuck you all night. But I've got a husband."

"That never stopped you before."

"I know, but I have to stop. This is goodbye."

"Are you sure?"

"Yeah, I have too much going on right now."

"Do you want to talk about it?"

"Not really."

"Shantell, you know, I'm in love with you."

"I got to go. Don't call anymore."

"So we can't even be friends?"

"Right." I got in my car and pulled off.

***

I found myself at Taraji's house. I knocked.

"Who is it?"

"Me."

She opened the door and looked me up and down. "What's wrong?"

I put my head on her shoulders and broke down crying.

"It's okay," she said. "What's going on?"

"I broke up with Darrell."

"So you called it off? That's good thing, right?"

"Tell it to my heart. I'm torn between them."

"Damn, Shantell, how did you get caught up like this?"

"I'm not even sure."

"It's going to be okay."

"I hope so."

"Come on, let's go smoke a blunt."

"Damn, I need it bad too."

"So what happened?"

"He called me and we met at Houston's. I fucked him in his car."

"Outside the restaurant?"

"Yeah."

"That dick must be fire?"

"Then I told him it was over with. I got in my car and pulled off with my head all fucked up."

"Damn! Bitch, you got a love jones. Here, smoke."

"I know," I said, blowing the weed smoke out of my mouth and nose.

CHAPTER 17
Shantell
Four months later

Baldwin had called me the day before to set up an appointment. "Have you been getting my texts?" he began.

"Yes."

"So why haven't you been answering?"

"For what? You keep asking the same shit."

"This isn't a joke."

"I know this."

"What have you decided? The prosecutor's been all over me about getting a decision from you."

"Nothing yet."

"Nothing. The trial is less than two weeks aways."

"I know."

"You know that they'll put Keith back in jail?"

"You know they're dead wrong for that shit."

"This is the government; they don't play fair."

"I see."

"Take a vacation with your family. You're too stressed."

"You think? I got all this shit on my plate. Pressure from you and the prosecutor. Fuck all this shit; I should have left Keith's ass in prison."

"I hear you. But they have to have answers."

"I'll let you know."' "Shantell, remember, nothing is more important than family.

"I know."

I got in my car and lit a blunt. My fucking nerves were bad as a motherfucker. I was fucked either way I decided.

Maybe I did need a family trip.

***

I decided to take my family to Dallas to Hurricane Harbor Wave Pools. They have a wide variety of pools that are all inside.

You can swim year round.

The kids were excited to try all the activities, so I told them, "Be back here in four hours. At 4:00, make your way to the front gate."

They ran off.

"I'm going to walk around and look," my mother said.

"Same thing: front gate, four hours.

"Will do...if I don't find a cutie."

"Whatever!"

Keith and I walked around the park. We were just eating and talking.

"I'm glad you planned this trip. We needed it," Keith said.

"No kidding."

"I've been too caught up in my work. I haven't been spending real time with you or the kids. I promise to make it up to y'all."

"I know, baby."

"I was thinking we could head back to the hotel for a quickie."

"Maybe we can go to a movie instead. You digging me?"

We sat at the top of the theater. No one else was near us. I unzipped Keith's pants and began playing with his dick. We used to do shit like this when we first met, but it had been a minute.

I went down on him, giving him head. I sucked on the tip of his dick and licked his balls. I felt him grab a handful of my hair.

"Yes, suck this dick."

I stopped and pulled my shorts down. I wasn't wearing any panties. My pussy was soaking wet. I grinded my pussy on him. The shit felt so good that I came all over.

He gripped my ass cheeks and bounced me on his dick until he started to shake. He filled my pussy with his cum.

"I love you."

"I love you back."

We stayed for two weeks and had a ton of fun. I left my phone off. I didn't want anyone to bother me. I wanted to spend time bonding with my family. Those two weeks with my family were wonderful.

As we were about to leave, Keith dropped to his knee.

"What are you doing?" It surprised me.

He pulled out a red box which held a big diamond ring.

My heart was pounding. It was like his first proposal.

"Shantell, I love you. You held a nigga down through everything. You stuck by my side and never left me. You've taken care of our kids and me. Will you marry me again?"

I looked at him and my kids and my mother. I knew I was a low down bitch. I had been doing bullshit, like what I did to get him out of prison and for sleeping with another man. I had to end that shit. My guilt hit me hard.

Tear were steaming down my face. I really wanted to confess everything. If he knew the bitch I'd become, he would kill me rather than marry me. They might eventually find my body in the river.

"What's wrong? Why are you crying?" he asked.

"Nothing."

"You sure you're okay?"

I wanted to tell him what a trifling bitch I had been. I was snorting coke and smoking weed. I kept falling for a man who had me dick whipped. But I didn't want to fuck up our trip. "These are happy tears. I'm so happy you are out of prison and we're all together. Of course I'll marry you again."

He slid the ring on my finger and stood up to hug and kiss me.

I still felt like shit.

Robert Baptiste

CHAPTER 18
Keith
Six months later

I sat in my office going over my books, making sure everything was straight with my company. I was waiting for the mayor to come see me. The city was getting ready to rebuild condos all over the city and build another hospital. I was trying to get one of them contracts. I needed to help my company. I had been getting a couple contracts, but I needed a major one. I hope me going to prison don't fuck shit up for me.

"Mr. Washington, the mayor is here."

"Thanks, Betty, show him in." I stood up, fixing my gray suit.

The mayor walked into the office wearing a dark blue suite and matching gators. He was short and brown-skinned with a bald head. I knew him from way back when he was a lawyer.

I came from around my desk and shook his hand. "Glad you came. Have a seat," I said.

"Well, we go way back, so I came to see what you were talking about."

I sat behind my desk and looked him straight in the eyes. "Well, Mayor, I need to get one of them city contract to help my business."

"Well, I see where the other mayor gave you a project for the first hospital and you went to prison on some federal charges."

"Well, I know I fucked that up, but it's all good now."

"Are you sure? Because I don't need the Feds in my shit."

"Yes, it's all out the way."

"How do I know if I give you this contract that you won't let me down?"

"I won't. You got my word."

"I don't know."

"I can do it cheaper than everybody."

"That might be so. But I don't need the Feds knocking at my door because I did you a favor."

"Hold up. I'm not no snitch. You already know. I'm a stand-up guy. I got out on my appeal and my charges got dropped."

"Let me think about it."

"Okay," I said, standing up and shaking his hand again.

"Later." He walked out.

I sat back in my chair, slamming my hand on the table. "Shit! I knew this shit was going to come back and bite me in the ass.

***

Shantell

I pulled up to the salon to meet with Icy. I hadn't seen her in a minute. I wanted to see her because I hadn't seen her since Keith got of jail. I was way too busy dealing with all the bullshit. Plus since we came back off vacation, all them promises Keith made to me, that shit went out the window. We were not even having sex.

I sat down next to Icy as the old Chinese women did pedicures on us.

"What's been up, stranger? You can't holla at a bitch since your dick came home?" Icy asked.

"Nothing like that. I've been busy being a mother and wife."

"I see. You look stressed out."

"Girl, I have a lot on my plate."

"You want to talk about it?"

"It's nothing serious. Just trying to get my life back," I lied.

"How is everyone?"

"The kids are good. Keith been trying to get this damn company off the ground."

"Shit, I thought y'all would have three more kids by now."

"Shit, lately, we barely fucking. It's been two months."

"At one point, y'all were fucking like rabbits."

"He's so caught up in his company that he doesn't have time to spend with me. But enough of my bullshit. What's going on with you?"

"Still living the single life. I been fucking with the check life."

"Bitch, you better be careful."

"I know. But bitch, I still need to eat out on these streets."

"I know. What's up with the girls?"

"Girl, those hoes are off doing their own things."

"I hear that." I didn't want to tell her that her life might be in danger because she was fucking with me. The same went for the rest of those whores. A bitch might be riding with me when my car exploded. The cartel was after me.

After our nails were finished, we went to the mall. I should tell her the truth, but I didn't need her to freak out in the mall.

"So when was the last time you sucked on some pussy?" Icy asked.

"It's been a minute. I haven't been getting no dick on the regular."

"You should go to his job and surprise him. If that don't work, bring your pussy back home. I still know a few tricks."

"I hear you." We hugged, and I left.

***

I pulled up at Keith's company. I took my panties off, then got out of the car. If the dick wouldn't come home, I'd bring the pussy to it.

When I walked in, he was talking on the phone. I took it from him and hung it up.

"What are you doing?"

"They'll call back." I tongue kissed him as I unzipped his pants. I dropped to my knees and I put his hard dick in my mouth. I sucked on it as I played with my pussy. As he moaned, I licked the precum from his dick.

I stood and bent over his desk. He raised my skirt and slammed his dick into my soaking wet pussy. He grabbed me by the shoulders as he thrust into me.

"Fuck this pussy!" I yelled, cumming all over his dick.

He picked me up, pinning me against the wall, and drove his dick into my pussy.

As I came back, he started to shake. "I'm cumming!" he

shouted.

"Me too."

He shot his hot nut into me. He let me down. We each tried to catch our breath.

"Damn, that was why you came here?"

"I've been needing some for a minute, but you've been at work. So I figured that if the dick wouldn't come home, I'd bring the pussy to it."

"I'm glad you did. I needed it too. I'm sorry, but I've been so busy trying to get my company off the ground."

"I know. I respect you for it."

"I love you."

"Love back." We kissed again. "Come with me."

"Yes, we can finish at home."

The phone rang.

"I got to get this."

"Okay."

"Alright, I'm on it," Keith said into the phone. "Baby, I'm going to have to take a raincheck." He kissed me and went back to the phone call.

I left with a half a smile on my face. See, that's the shit that makes me go back to Darrell. I don't like that one minute shit. Darrell always has time for me. I thought shit was going to be different when Keith and I got back from Dallas, but shit was still the same.

Keith had been different since getting out of jail. He always worked, but he used to be more fun and spontaneous. Now, all he wanted to do was come home and sleep.

I'm lucky if a bitch gets some dick. He kept promising to spend more time with me, but it only lasted a few moments. Then he went back to work nights and days.

CHAPTER 19
Shantell
Three weeks later

It was the day of Deloso's trial.

As I got out of bed, I fell to my knees to pray.

"Dear God, it's me. I'm asking you to be with me today. I know I haven't been your favorite person. I do a lot of things I shouldn't. But please watch out for my family and friends. Don't let no one harm them. Keep your hands on them. Don't make them pay for my sins. In Jesus's name, amen."

The night before, I had gone out to dinner with my family. I told everyone how much I loved them. At home, I fucked my husband like he had the last dick on earth.

I lit a blunt and took a hard pull. The trial was closed to the public. Nobody knew except Taraji and Baldwin.

As I got ready, Taraji called to tell me she was going to court with me. That's why I love that bitch. She's got my back no matter what.

The trial started at 9:00 a.m., a couple hours from now.

I sprayed on Dior perfume and put on a white Balmain dress with long sleeves. It was thigh-length. I added some white Manolo Blahnik shoes. I added a little makeup and red lipstick.

I was glad that Keith and the kids were already gone so I didn't have to answer any questions. Keith had left early to go to work. He was trying to be a good husband, but my trifling ass was out here cheating and putting his life in jeopardy with my dumb choices and bad decisions.

I needed to get my shit together, for real.

I called Taraji from my black Bentley to tell her I'd be there in a minute.

I honked at the curb in front of her house. She came out wearing a green and white Zimmerman miniskirt, Messika jewelry, and green Manolo Blahnik shoes. She got in the car.

"What do you got on? It smells good," I asked.

"It's my new Tiffany's perfume."

"I need to get some of that. Thanks for coming with me."

"No problem. You're my best friend. We'll get through this." She gripped my hand.

As we drove to the courthouse, Baldwin called to ask where I was at.

"This motherfucker keeps asking me if I'm on my way," I complained.

"Who?"

"This fucking lawyer. I'm not talking to him anymore. I didn't even want to do this shit."

"What made you change your mind?"

"I thought about it. I don't need this motherfucker knocking on my door to arrest my husband. I don't need no more bullshit in my life."

"That's for damn sure. You doing the right thing. You have to keep your family safe."

"That's what I keep telling myself."

"You got this."

"I hope you're right."

As soon as I saw the courthouse, I got butterflies in my stomach.

"Bitch, what's wrong with you?" Taraji asked.

"Bitch, I hate coming here. Every time I come here, I get so nervous that it feels like I got to shit."

"Bitch, I smell you."

"My bad, I farted."

We walked up the stairs.

"Bitch, I didn't know this was a federal building and I've lived in New Orleans all my life!" Taraji exclaimed.

"Me either. It goes to show that we don't know New Orleans like we think we do."

"Bitch, I passed this building a million times. I still didn't know it was federal."

At the metal detector, we emptied our pockets and walked to the elevator. We got off on the fifth floor. I saw signs pointing to a courtroom.

"I got to go to the bathroom. The courtroom is over there. Go on in. I'll be there in a minute," I said.

"I'm coming with you. Being in this motherfucker has me nervous too."

The bathroom was large. There were marble countertops and black-lacquered stalls. Everything seemed almost too clean.

I sat on the toilet to take a shit. I pulled out a little mirror and poured a line of coke on it. I rolled up a twenty and snorted a fat line.

"Bitch, are you snorting in there?" Taraji asked.

"Bitch, I can't do this shit sober."

"Pass me some?"

I slid her the mirror and coke and heard her snort the rest of it.

We washed our hands, using the mirrors to be sure everything was fine.

"Bitch, I feel better now," I said.

"After this, bitch, I need to get drunk and laid. I don't even care with whom. I'm stressed out, and I don't even have to testify."

"Now you know how I feel. Let's go. Baldwin texted me again."

***

The courtroom was cold as a motherfucker. It gave me chills. Almost nobody was there. Although this was the biggest trial in the history of New Orleans, it was closed to the public. I was glad it was that way.

The room was large, and didn't look like a state courtroom. At State, people ran around making a lot of noise. Shit looked raggedy. Here, the floor was blue carpet. There were big skinny wooden benches and white leather chairs for the jury.

Baldwin and the prosecutor came up.

"I'm glad you made it," Baldwin started.

"I started not to come to this shit."

"I'm glad you did. Well, sit here behind the prosecutor."

Sandra Lewis was wearing a light blue skirt and button-down

blouse with white pumps. She was handling the case herself. She didn't want to lose.

"I'm glad to see you. Everything will be okay," she said.

The jury came in. There were six old white women, three old black men, and three old Mexican women. They looked like they spent all their time watching the news all day long. They saw how all this drug shit killed people, so they couldn't wait to send a motherfucker to prison for the rest of his life.

The bailiff and a U.S. Marshal entered. "All rise. This court is in session for the eastern district of Louisiana. Judge Balls is presiding."

Everyone got up. A short bald black man with a neatly-trimmed beard came in wearing a black robe. He sat down, staring around the courtroom.

"You may be seated."

Two white Marshals bought in Deloso. He was wearing a black suit and black loafers. He had no handcuffs or shackles on. As he walked by me, he had a serious death look on his face. It sent chills down my spine. I'm glad I was high in this bitch. If I wasn't, I would've walked out.

They took him over to his lawyers. It got so quiet in the courtroom that you could hear a rat piss on cotton.

Taraji leaned forward and whispered, "Bitch, that nigga look like he shouldn't be fucked with."

"You're right. This shit for real. That's why I've been scared. This nigga don't play."

The judge called the court to order.

The prosecutor rose. "Ladies and gentlemen of the jury, we will prove that Mr. Deloso is the head of the Gulf Coast Cartel, has killed federal agents, and has distributed more than a ton of cocaine to New Orleans and other Gulf states. He's to blame for an unbelievable amount of drugs entering the country. He callously kills anyone who works against these interests. He is the most feared cartel boss in the world. We have a lot of witnesses coming to speak, despite the fact that it may put their lives in danger. Mr. Deloso reached from one prison to another to kill Eric

Hampton, another witness in this case. You must remove Mr. Deloso from the streets for the rest of his life. Thank you."

Deloso's lawyer stood to talk. I have heard that they're the best money can buy.

"Ladies and gentlemen, the prosecutor spins a fairy tale of drugs and murder. My client is simply a businessman caught up in the unfair mechanizations of an all-powerful federal government. He is basically accused of being successful and a minority. That's certainly no crime. The government will present a series of witnesses who are all in trouble and saw a way out by wrongly and unfairly blaming Mr. Deloso."

"Will the United States call its first witness?" the judge asked.

I nervously took the stand and took an oath to "tell the truth, the whole truth, and nothing but the truth" with my hand on the bible.

"Mrs. Washington, what is your relationship with the Gulf Coast Cartel?"

"I worked for Deloso by selling drugs in New Orleans."

"And who else were you working for?"

"I worked undercover for the federal government in an effort to arrest him."

"Did you see Mr. Deloso commit a homicide?" Ms. Lewis asked.

Deloso gave me a "bitch, you are so dead" look.

"Yes, several times."

Ms. Lewis put up a picture. "Tell the court what happen to this DEA agent."

"Mr. Deloso killed him with a baseball bat."

"Tell the jury how much cocaine you were moving for Deloso."

"I was moving 2000 kilos a month."

"No further questions," She walked back to her table.

Deloso's attorney got up. "Mrs. Washington, why did you start working for the Feds."

"My husband was in prison."

"So your actions were done to frame my client?"

"Objection!" the prosecutor yelled.

"Sustained. Move on."

"Did you play a role in the death of the DEA agent?"

"Objection. Assumes facts not in evidence."

"Overruled. Please answer, the question?"

"I shot him, but – "

"One could say that you killed him, right?"

"No, he was already dead."

"No further questions."

I looked at Deloso. He mouthed that I was a dead nigga bitch.

I went back to my section. I felt bad. It was like I was being judged.

***

Over the next few days, I watched as the prosecutor presented nearly a hundred witnesses. The defense countered with about twenty of their own. Finally, the judge dismissed the jury to deliberate.

I decided to leave. Baldwin said he would call when the verdict came in. Taraji and I left to get some food.

"Bitch, light that blunt. I need to calm my nerves," I said.

Keith called. "I just wanted to tell you I love you."

"I love you too."

"My plug's been on trial all this week."

"I heard."

"I'm glad they chose not to indict me along with him."

"Me too."

As he hung up, Baldwin called. "The verdict is in," he said.

"I'm on my way."

"What happened?" Taraji asked

"The jury is back."

"Already?"

"Yes."

"Damn, that was fast."

"I know."

We got back to court just as the jury re-entered the room. The jury foreman gave the bailiff a piece of paper. The bailiff handed it to the judge who read it.

"Has the jury reached a verdict?"

"Yes, Your Honor. We, the jury, find Mr. Deloso guilty of conspiracy to distribute drugs and conspiracy to commit murder."

The Marshals put Deloso back in handcuffs.

He looked at me. "You're dead, bitch. You and your family."

I got goosebumps. I turned to the prosecutor.

She said. "Don't worry about him. He'll spend the rest of his life at a super max in Florence."

"I'm not worried. I'm good." But I was feeling a little spooked as I pulled off.

"How do you really feel?" asked Taraji.

"Bitch, roll something up."

"I got you." She pulled a blunt from the glove compartment and lit it. She passed it to me after a couple of puffs. I took a long pull.

"Bitch, did you see the look that motherfucker gave me?" I asked.

"Hell yeah."

"Bitch, it looked like he wanted to kill me right there."

"I'm glad the Marshals was there. That motherfucker scared me too. I'm glad that shit's over. Now you can move on with your life. And Keith don't have to know."

"I know."

"Let's go celebrate."

"Sounds good." I put on my best fake smile.

Deep down, I knew this shit wasn't finished. This motherfucker wouldn't let it go that easy.

As we drove around the city, I felt like I had signed a death warrant for everyone I knew.

We parked at the lake, smoked and snorted coke, then I dropped Taraji off at home.

At home, I stripped, got in the tub, and was determined to get high. I put more coke on my mirror and snorted it up.

"Fuck, I needed that shit," I said, snorting another line.

I lay back in the tub, feeling the high come over me.

I was still afraid. I didn't want to die. I just wanted my husband out of prison.

I went to bed and fell into a deep sleep.

Talking awoke me. "You black nigga bitch. You thought I couldn't get you? I'm Deloso."

I awoke from a dream. Sweat dripped from my body. *Damn, it felt real*, I thought.

CHAPTER 20
Deloso
One month later

The Marshals walked me back into the courtroom. This time I was in a belly chain and shackles. They had closed the courtroom during my trial. I still couldn't believe that bitch told on me after everything I did for her and her husband. I made that broke bitch a millionaire, and this was how she thanked me. I stood in front of the judge.

"Mr. Deloso, you are here today for sentencing. You were found guilty of conspiracy to distribute cocaine, conspiracy to commit homicide, and homicide. Do you understand what is happening today?"

"Yes, Your Honor, he does," my lawyer said.

"Your client needs to acknowledge it."

I looked at him with death in my eyes. I would kill his ass when I got out of this shit.

"I said, do you understand?" he repeated.

I stayed silent.

"Okay, I have carefully considered your case. Given the lawlessness you have fostered across New Orleans and the rest of the United States and that you have been found guilty by jury of your peers, I hereby sentence you to four life sentences in a maximum security federal prison."

"Your Honor, the defense will be filing an appeal immediately," my lawyer said.

"As is your right. Until then. Mr. Deloso will be held in custody of the U.S. government in Florence, Colorado."

The Marshalls took me back to a holding cell.

I had to come up with a plan. I was not going to spend the rest of my life in prison. They must not know who I am.

My lawyer came by the holding cell. "Do you need me to do anything?"

"Talk to my brother."

"Okay, boss, I'm on it."

The tray slot opened at 2:00 a.m. A guard on my payroll handed me a cell phone, some Mexican food, and a newspaper from Mexico. The drug trade had been getting out of hand since my arrest. The other cartels wanted to steal my business. They knew I was given four life sentences. They didn't know I would be back.

I called my brother. He was my second-in-command, but nobody can run your business like you do. "What's going on out there?" I asked.

"We're at war with other cartels, especially the Zetas. They want our spot."

"Those motherfuckers were working for us. What happened?"

"They got a new leader. He wants to show the other cartels that he's not fucking around."

"Who is he?"

"Santiago Robles."

"I know him. He reminds me of me. Hernandez, hold it together until I get out of this bitch."

"I am."

"I need you to put hits on everyone who's even remotely involved with my case. I need you to find that nigga bitch and her husband and send them a message."

"I'm on it."

"Don't let me down."

"I won't. I promise that everyone's who's involved with you going to jail is dead."

"That's what I wanted to hear. Love you."

"Love you, bro."

CHAPTER 21
Shantell
Five months later

Icy and I were in Victoria's Secret helping me look for some sexy lingerie. My sex life was non-existent. I was trying not to call Darrell's ass. I didn't need no more drama in my life. I got enough of that shit going on.

"Them are cute."

"You like this pink thong?"

"It's cute. Did you take my advice?"

"Yes."

"So how it went?"

"Girl, I went over to Keith's job like you said."

"And?"

"We fucked."

"That's a good thing, right?"

"Bitch, it lasted every bit of thirty seconds."

"Damn! Keith doing it like that?"

"His phone rang. And he told me we was going to finish at the house."

"Well, did y'all?"

"Bitch, he came home and went straight to sleep."

"Damn!"

"Girl, I think I'm losing my mojo. And my man."

"You don't think he's cheating on you?"

"No, he just caught up in the damn company."

"Well, look like to me you need to spice it up."

"Threesomes always work."

"Well, we ain't had one in a minute. That might just do the trick."

"Holla at me. I'm always down to do a threesome with you and Keith."

***

Shantell

At the restaurant, Keith and I sat at a table eating shrimp and steak with red wine. I had told him I needed to go out on a date. We hadn't been on a date in years. Plus I threw in his face what he told me in Dallas.

"Shantell, I know I haven't been spending much time with you."

"You sure haven't."

"And I'm sorry."

"As you should be."

"But the company been keeping me busy."

"What about me? I have needs."

"I know."

"It's been two months and you haven't touched me."

"I'm sorry for that."

"What is it?" I'm not attractive to you anymore?"

"No, I don't want you to every think that. You are beautiful to me."

"You sure don't make me feel like it. Are you cheating on me?"

"Hell no."

"So you still love me?"

He reached over took both my hands, kissed them. "I never stop loving you."

"Are you sure?"

He smiled.

"Why are you smiling?"

"Because I never stopped. You my girl for life." He pulled out a black box. He handed it to me.

I opened it up and it was a diamond necklace.

"You like it?"

"I love it."

I came around the table, hugging and kissing him.

"Let's go home."

***

Back at the house, as soon as we walked through the door Icy walked up to us butt-naked. She was still built like a brick house, red and thick, very big ass and nice-sized titties. I had this set up because I was trying to save my marriage and get me some much-needed dick and pussy.

"What's this?" Keith smiled.

"Well, you gave me a surprise, I thought I'd do one better."

"You sure right."

"Plus we need this."

"Let's go upstairs," Icy said, taking Keith by the hand.

We took his clothes off of him as we took turns sucking on his hard dick. She sucked on his balls while I sucked and licked on his dick.

"Damn! Y'all give fire head."

We stopped, letting him watch us eat each other out. We 69'ed each other as he sat in the chair stroking his dick.

He slid back into bed as Icy climbed on top of him, riding his dick as I watched and played with my pussy.

"I'm cumming, Keith," she said, shaking.

I climbed on top, riding his dick as he ate Icy's pussy out. I came all over his dick. He put my legs on his shoulders and stuck his dick in me. He fucked me hard and deep as I dug my nails into his back.

"Fuck! I love you," I said, cumming back to back while Icy sucked on my titties

We both got in the doggy-style position, letting him fuck each of us from behind. I watched sweat drip off his body as he hit her from the back. He looked so good that it turned me on even more. He was back to the Keith I knew.

He slide his dick out of Icy and I slid it in my asshole.

I wanted him to fuck me in every one of my holes tonight. That's how I was feeling.

He gripped my ass cheeks, thrusting his dick in and out of me as Icy played with my clit. My body started tensing up. Getting hit in the ass is a whole different climax. It's hard and tense.

I grabbed the sheet with my eyes closed tight as my body starting to shake out of control.

"Fuck! I'm cumming." I came so hard back to back, I had the whole bed wet. That shit came out of me like a waterfall. And it was much needed.

We laid in Keith's arms, each of us catching our breath.

"Baby, you enjoyed it?"

"Just like old times."

CHAPTER 22
One year later
Sandra

As the water streamed over me, I reflected on how good the last year had been. I was the frontrunner to become New Orleans's next mayor. Convicting Deloso and getting him four life sentences had helped my campaign. All the polls said I was winning. I was going to be the first black woman mayor ever in New Orleans. Just thinking about it made my nipples hard and my pearl tongue swollen.

I hadn't had sex in a minute. It had been about two years. I needed to find a man.

I slid my finger on my pearl tongue. I rubbed it as I squeezed on my hard nipples with the other. I bit my bottom lip. It felt so good. I closed my eyes tight, moaning in pleasure.

"Fuck, fuck! I'm cumming. I'm cumming!" My knees buckled as I came back to back. It took some effort to keep myself from falling.

As I was regaining my composure, I heard my phone ringing. I got out of the shower, quickly wrapped a towel around me, and went to the bedroom to answer my phone.

As I was answering, the doorbell rang. I wasn't expecting anyone.

"Hello?"

"This is Stan Brown. We have a major problem." Brown was an FBI agent

"I'll have to call you back. Someone's at the door."

I put on a robe and saw a tall, dark chocolate bald man wearing a blue suit.

"I'm Bobby Smith. I'm an FBI agent. There's a problem."

"Come in." Damn, he smelled good, and he was fine, too. "What's up?"

"Members of the jury panel are being killed."

My phone rang again. "What, Stan?"

"There's a big problem,"

"Agent Smith is explaining it to me."

"Good. Got to go."

Agent Smith continued, "Several members of the Deloso jury are either dead or missing. We just found two of them murdered in their houses. They were shot twice in the back of their heads."

"What?" My heart skipped a beat.

"Are you all right?"

"Fuck. We need to warn the rest of the jury."

"We're working on it, but can't find all of them. Agents are out looking for them."

"Is the Gulf Coast Cartel responsible?"

"I've investigated them for years. They'll target everyone involved in the case like this."

"Shit, that won't look good."

"We're putting police on you."

"Good. Keep me informed."

He left, and I locked the door. I paced as I worried about the options.

We can't ask people to come forward and help us if we can't protect them. I was partly to blame. Deloso was still in New Orleans, pending appeal. I kept him here. I could see the headlines now: "Prosecutor allows cartel boss to remain in city" and "Jurors in Deloso case found murdered".

Tomorrow, the mayor, the media, and everyone else would be asking questions that I didn't have good answers for.

I had planned to smoke a joint and fantasize about Morris Chestnut's fine ass. Damn, I'd like to drink his bathwater. Dreams were out, but I needed the joint and a drink.

I poured a Jack straight and went to my bedroom and got a joint out of my nightstand. As I smoked and drank, I wondered what the fuck I'd say to the press tomorrow.

***

At the office, my best friend Anna came up to me. "Sandra, is it true? Have members of the jury been coming up dead and missing?"

Anna was sexy with caramel skin and long black hair. Her face was freckled and she had hazel eyes. She had been raised in New Orleans. She was French-speaking Creole. She looked a little like Kerry Washington.

We had met at Harvard Law. We were in the program at the same time. What really made us jam was that we are both from the eastern part of New Orleans.

She went to St. Mary's while I went to John Mac.

"Yeah, I think my ass is on fire because of it. My poll numbers are down. Now I have to go see Frank."

"Good luck."

"I'm going to need it."

In my office. Frank's secretary came down to get me.

I spent a couple of minutes trying to get my thoughts together. I knew I was in for a grilling. I figured Frank was going to remind me that I had asked for the case, and he gave it to me against his better judgement. Fuck that. I'd worked for the Federal Prosecutor's office for fifteen years. I was passed over for the head prosecutor's office twice. I had a better resume than most. Plus, I was running for mayor. I didn't need this.

I grabbed a strawberry candy and took the elevator to Frank's floor. When I got to Frank's office he was on the phone. Agent Smith was there. I wondered why. I found myself curious as to whether or not he had a girlfriend. Fine as he was, he was probably married. The fine ones tend to be married, gay, or just whores. I sat down next to him in a black leather chair in front of a glass table. The brother smelled good too.

There were pictures of Frank's white wife and mixed-race kids. His office was filled with his medals and trophies. The window gave him a prime view of New Orleans.

Frank was light-skinned. He was about 6'2" with black wavy hair. He was wearing black slacks and a white dress shirt. He had taken off his tie and undone the top button on his shirt. He had transferred from D.C. to become the Federal District Attorney. The mayor of the city asked the Feds to step in and help with the police corruption and the big drug and murder problem they had in the city.

Frank looked at me. He seemed frustrated. He slammed the phone down. "I've been on the phone with Washington since 3 a.m. trying to explain to the AG about federal jurors being slaughtered. The news media is eating this shit up, claiming we can't protect the citizens. They're saying that jurors are being led like cows to a slaughter house. I knew you couldn't handle this case."

"Are you saying I got them killed?"

"It's your case. Where do you think they got the jurors' addresses from?"

"What are you saying?"

"Do I need to spell it out for you?"

"You damn well need to."

"Somebody on your team is leaking information."

"Why it can't be in the Bureau?"

"Watch yourself."

"Okay, stop this. It's not productive," Agent Smith interrupted.

"Have you contacted the rest of the jurors?" Frank asked.

"We are working on it," Agent Smith said. His phone rang. "I'm on my way."

"What's going on?" Frank asked.

"They found another juror's body."

"Fuck!" Frank slammed his hand on his desk. "What happened?"

"Didn't say."

"Keep me posted."

"Will do, sir." He left.

Frank turned back to me. "You need to figure out what you're going to say to the press. I'm not taking the heat for this clusterfuck. Try to get in contact with your witnesses. Can you handle that?"

"Yes, sir." I left his office.

Anna came in as I was back at my desk. "What's happening?"

"Close the door."

She complied. "So what happened?"

"I got my ass chewed out. Everything's on me. He even said someone on my team gave the cartel the jurors' addresses. Can you believe that shit?"

"That's crazy. Don't they know those motherfuckers have long arms?"

"Well, Frank can kiss my ass. Fuck him."

"So now what?"

"I have to hold a press conference and call the witnesses. Their lives could be in danger too."

"Isn't your star witness still in the city?"

"Shantell Washington? Oh shit, I really need to check on her." I picked up the phone and dialed her cell number.

***

Agent Smith

I pulled up to the scene on Magazine Street in the uptown area. The blue car and upstairs of the house was sealed with red and yellow tape. The scene was flooded with NOPD offices and FBI agents. I showed my FBI credentials to the officer guarding the area, and he waved me through.

Two people had been killed in a car. They looked young. Each had been shot twice in the head. It looked like a mob hit.

I walked upstairs. "Who's in charges?"

"I'm the SAC. Stan Brown. FBI."

"Bobby Smith. I'm from the District Bureau."

"You here to oversee the case?"

"Yes. What's going on?"

"A blood bath. They killed the entire family. Husband and wife are in the bedroom. Kids coming back from college were killed in the car. They even shot their dog."

"Were they jurors in the Deloso case?"

"Yeah, Katherine Richards was the juror, and the other victim is her husband Bill."

I went to the bedroom. They were lying across the bed. Their throats were cut, and each had been shot twice in the back of the head. Obviously, the cartel meant to kill everyone.

"I've seen this before when I tried to stop a war between cartels. We just made things worse. When you take the boss of bosses out, the rest go to war to see who will replace him. Are there any witnesses? Did anyone see anything?"

"Nobody claims to have heard a sound."

"I know why. They use silencers."

"Who?"

"The cartel. This is their work. I have been following them for ten years now. They keep an assassin in the U.S. for these situations."

"Will they kill everyone involved in this case?"

"They'll certainly try."

"How did they found out where the jurors stayed?"

"My guess is somebody on the inside."

"That's crazy."

"Millions of dollars will make you turn on your own mother."

"Millions?"

"They pay top dollar for info."

"Damn."

"Well, I'm out. Keep me posted."

"Got you."

I called Frank from the car. "Another family dead. The Richards and their kids. Throats were cut. Double tapped. Shot in the back of the head. They even killed the dog."

"Shit! Stay on top of it."

"I'm on it."

***

Sandra

I was nervous as I prepared to face the media. Reporters from all over the state and city were outside Camp Street awaiting answers. Another juror had been killed. Shit had been going sideways. The mayor had been pestering Frank. I had to keep hearing that. A bitch really needed a joint right now. I knew I was on the hit list. I needed to have my car checked and get extra security.

Shantell didn't answer her phone. I hoped she wasn't dead. As I left my office, Bobby was coming up the hallway. Damn, he was hot. I hoped he would give a bitch some dick. "Where are you going?" I asked. "With you." "To the press circus?" "Frank wanted me there." "I'm glad you're with me." "I wouldn't have it any other way."

I smiled as we left the building to shouting questions and flashing cameras. I walked over to the small podium set up for the conference. "Everyone please be quiet," I started.

Bobby and I were joined by a few federal agents, Frank, and a few other prosecutors. My hands, armpits, and everything else were sweating. It didn't help that it was the middle of the summer, and New Orleans is hot. My stomach was in a knot. I needed to practice speaking in public if I was going to be mayor. Politics is mainly lying to people to give them hope that the city will get better.

I began, "You've heard about the recent murders of jurors in New Orleans. It is our job to protect them, but so far, we have failed. We are taking proactive steps to resolve this. We've gotten every law enforcement agency involved, and we're putting witnesses and jurors in protective custody until we get it resolved. We ask the public for a little patience. I will take a few questions."

"Do you know who is responsible?" "We have some solid leads." "Who are you looking at?" "I can't say while the investigation is ongoing." "Is the Gulf Coast Cartel involved?" "We're still looking into that."

"When will you know more?"

"When we finish the investigation."

"Are you a target?"

"That's enough," Frank said. We left the podium and returned inside the building. "You did good. I'm proud," Frank said as he went to his office.

"You did good." Anna hugged me.

"Great job. Want to grab a drink?" Bobby asked.

"Yeah, it's been a long day. Let me put my stuff up. I'll meet you at my car.

"Okay."

I was glad he asked. He might get some pussy if he talked right and didn't say no stupid shit.

***

"Fuck yeah! Give me that dick."

I was lying on my stomach as he slammed his dick in my soaking wet pussy. I had cum a couple of times before we even got to the house. The brother knew how to talk to a lady.

He had been married once before, but didn't have any kids. He was from Dallas, Texas. And he had a nice-sized eight inch dick and knew how to work it.

"Fuck! I'm cumming again." I put my head into the pillow while shaking.

He turned me over on my back and put my legs over my shoulders. I didn't care what he did as long as he kept drilling me with his dick. My pussy squirted all over his dick as he thrust in me.

"Fuck, this pussy is good. Nice and tight."

I guess it'd been so long that I was like a virgin.

"Yes, daddy, give it to me."

I raised my ass up in the air as he gripped my cheeks and pulled my hair, slamming his dick into me. I slammed my ass against his dick as he started shaking, shooting all of his hot nut in my pussy as I came again all over his dick. The Lord must know that I needed a man.

He hit all the right spots and had me cumming like never before. Even my cheating-ass husband never put it on me like that.

A bitch was so drained that I fell asleep in our cum and sweat.

Robert Baptiste

CHAPTER 23
Shantell

I got off the interstate in Houston. I was heading downtown to Darrell's condo. I know what I had said, but he's like a drug to me. I can't get him out of my system, not with the way he fucks me. I cum so hard that it's a shame.

We'd been having sex again for the last two months. We hooked up when I came to Houston to check up on one of the beauty shops I had opened in the area. He kept calling me, but I ignored him. Then I got to feeling bad about how I had ended it with him. We went out to eat. The next thing I knew, we were fucking at his condo.

Beside, Keith and I hadn't been fucking. He's too caught up in trying to get his new company started. He's been too busy to make time for me. We haven't had sex in the last three months. When we do, it's fifteen minutes and that's on a good night. It's maybe because he's working too hard, but I got needs.

I had hit Brittney up and was trying to kick it with her, but the bitch wasn't in. She was doing good out there. She had opened a strip club in the Southwest.

The prosecutor told me Deloso was on his appeal, but it wouldn't do any good. I was glad. Fuck him. I thought I'd be walking on pins and needles. I thought shit would keep blowing up around me. They would kidnap and kill my kids and then Keith and then me. But shit was cool now. No threats or deliveries.

I pulled up at Darrell's condo, pulled off my thong, and got out. I knocked and he answered with nothing on but a hard dick.

I stroked his dick while kissing him. He picked me up, pinned me to the wall, and thrust his dick in me.

"Fuck, I'm cumming," I said as I held him tight.

"Fuck, this pussy good."

"Y-y-yes! Fuck me! I'm cumming."

He carried me to his bedroom and threw me on the bed. He put my legs on his shoulders thrusting in me, beating my walls up. It felt like he was in my stomach. I loved every minute of it. I got on top of him, riding him like a horse. He grabbed my ass and bounced me up and down on his dick. I shook as I came, digging my nails into his chest.

He flipped me on my stomach. As he thrust inside me, he bit my neck as I came back to back. I got on all fours, letting him hit me from the back as he pulled my hair.

"Fuck, I'm cumming," I moaned.

"Me too."

I felt him shaking as he shot his hot nut in my pussy. I fell on to the bed with his dick still in me. We tried to catch our breaths.

As he pulled his dick out, I was still cumming. Lord, this man can fuck. This was how it used to be with Keith and me. Playing around like this, a bitch might end up pregnant again.

"Why haven't you left that nigga yet?" he asked.

"I'm still in love with him.'

"Then why are you here with me?"

"Ain't it obvious?"

"No, tell me."

"You got some good dick."

"That's all?"

"I'm not leaving Keith."

"So where does that leave me?"

"My side dick."

"I want more."

"I told you when we started fucking again that I wouldn't leaving my husband. You said you were cool with that."

"Knowing you're going to leave me and go back to him, I can't take that."

My phone rang. I answered without thinking.

"Mrs. Washington? This is Sandra Lewis."

"What do you want? This is supposed to be finished."

"We need to talk. It's important."

"I'm done with that shit."

"You may be in danger."

"So?" I hung up.

Darrell asked, "Who was that?"

"A bill collector."

"Let's finish our conversation.'

"I don't want to talk." I crawled to him on my knees. I put his dick in my mouth.

"We can finish this later."

"That's what I was thinking."

I sucked on his shaved balls.

***

Back in New Orleans, the prosecutor was still trying to call. I didn't have shit to talk to them about. It had been a year since I testified against Deloso. I didn't have time for their bullshit.

I decided to call Keith to let him know I was back in town and see if he would be home early. He'd been so wrapped up in pursuing a city contract that he hadn't been coming home until the middle of the night.

"Baby," he answered his phone.

"I was calling to see if you wanted me to fix dinner?"

"No, I have tons of paperwork. I'll be late."

"I'll leave it in the microwave for you."

"Love you."

"Love you too."

That's the shit I'm talking about. He never made time for me anymore. That's why I'm getting dick from Darrell. At least that nigga has time for me.

There was an Amazon package outside my door. I didn't remember buying anything, but it was probably one of the kids'. I brought it inside and set it on the kitchen counter. I opened the box.

"What the fuck!" I screamed.

It was a box of dead rats with a letter: BITCH, IT'S YOUR FAMILY'S WORST NIGHTMARE. I'LL KILL YOU AND YOUR FAMILY.

I ran with the box to the backyard and threw it in the trash. I ran upstairs, rubbing my hands through my hair. My nerves were on edge. How did this motherfucker know where I lived? That meant my family was in danger.

How could I convince Keith we had to move immediately? It could have been a bomb. What had I got myself into? My family? My husband? I couldn't keep this secret much longer. If someone got killed, my conscience couldn't take it. I had to tell Keith.

I snorted a line of coke. I grabbed my black .38 and carried it to the pool. I lit a cigarette, taking a hard puff. I was supposed to be quitting.

This shit was really real now. What the fuck was I going to do?

***

As I was leaving my beauty shop the next day, I saw a Taurus parked next to my car. It was gray with dark tinted windows. It looked like an FBI car. Someone was inside. My heart pounded. My stomach turned. A thousand thoughts flooded my brain. I hoped nothing bad had happened to Keith or the kids. My head had been fucked up ever since I received that box. I was carrying my gun and checking my car for bombs. I didn't need any shit from the Feds.

As I walked toward my car, two black men got out and intercepted me.

"Mrs. Washington, we're with the FBI. We need a minute of your time." They displayed their badges.

"I have nothing I want to talk to you about."

"Be that as it may, we still need to talk to you."

"I didn't answer when you called. Just leave me alone."

"You don't have a choice. Show up at the Federal building tomorrow, or we'll bring you and your husband there."

"What is this about?"

"We'll talk tomorrow."

Ever since I got in bed with the government, my life had been fucked up. I should have left Keith's ass in prison.

When I got home, Keith was pulling up.

"Hey baby, you home early?" I said.

"Yeah, a little tried today. Did you hear about the Deloso case?"

"What about it?" I said, walking inside.

"It's breaking news. The jurors in Deloso's case are getting killed. I knew that shit would happen. You can't tell on a motherfucker like that and then think it's over. He's going to kill you."

I ran to the bathroom to throw up. How could he be out of prison? How was it even fucking possible?

I ran a bubble bath. I felt really sick. I needed something strong. I grabbed some coke and a blunt. I walked downstairs to grab a bottle of red wine.

"Baby, you good?" Keith asked.

"I'm just going to relax in a bubble bath. My stomach's a little upset."

"I'll join you in a minute."

"No, I just need to relax. I got a lot on my mind."

"Do you want to talk about it?"

"It's really nothing. Just something with the shops."

"Remember, you can talk to me about anything. I love you." He kissed me.

"I know, baby. Love you back."

I locked the bathroom door. I put some coke on the mirror and snorted a line. I hit the blunt and hit it deeply. I started drinking the wine straight from the bottle.

I used to be a good wife and mother. Now I was just a lying hoe and druggie and a no-good bitch who got all my family and friends into deep bullshit

FUCK. FUCK.

Robert Baptiste

CHAPTER 24
Shantell

I got up and got dressed the next morning. Fortunately, Keith and the kids were already gone. I went to the closet to grab some coke and weed. I had a few hours before I needed to be at the federal building.

In the parking lot, I snorted a line of coke. I needed to be high to deal with these motherfuckers. I checked the mirror to make sure my nose was clean. I got out of the car, fixing my white dress. I couldn't imagine what they wanted to see me about. I saw the shit on the news already.

I took the elevator to the third floor and was met by an older white Marshal. He escorted me to a conference room where I saw Baldwin, Sandra Lewis, and a couple of DEA agents.

"Damn, Baldwin. You weren't going to call me and tell me that motherfucker got out?"

Sandra Lewis interrupted, "He's not out. And we've tried to reach you for days."

"I don't want to talk to you. I was talking to my so-called lawyer."

"Shantell, I tried to call you. I even went by your house, but you weren't there."

Baldwin argued. "I had to go out of town on business."

"Have a seat," Sandra said.

"I'll stand."

"Here's what's going on."

"I've seen the news. Jurors and witnesses are being killed."

"Yes. But he's not out. He's sending hits from jail. And we feel that the lives of you and your family are in danger."

"What are you saying?"

"It's time for you to enter witness protection."

"Hell no!"

"Why not?"

"One: My husband still doesn't know about this shit y'all got me in. Two: I don't want him to know."

"You need to think about your family's safety rather than your secrets."

"I'm thinking about my family. Do you know what Keith will do to me?"

"Surely he would understand."

"Bitch, is you crazy? You've seen his rap sheet. You know what he can do. Remember, he scared y'all enough that y'all gave him thirty years. So no, that motherfucker will not understand. He will kill my ass."

"Do you really want to be on your own?"

"Yeah. I'd also appreciate it if you stop sending agents to my place of business."

"I told you she wouldn't go for it," Baldwin said. "You need to tell her."

"Tell me what?"

Sandra started, "The other reason why your family's lives are in danger. A letter was sent to my office. It said that you and your family are next on the list. You need to go into WITSEC until this over. We think we can protect you better that way. Or we could put people outside your house."

"It's too late for that. They already sent me a box of dead rats."

"When?"

"A couple of days ago."

"Mrs. Washington, you need to let us protect you."

"I'll think about it."

"At least let me put some agents near you."

"I have to find a way to tell my husband about this. I'll get back to you."

"Do that."

"I will."

I walked out with Baldwin on my heels. "Shantell, you need to think about this."

"I know."

"You need me to tell him?"

"Like that's going to make it easier? Once he finds out you

involved, he going to kill your ass too. What part of that shit don't you understand?"

"You right."

"Don't do shit."

"Call and let me know something."

"All right."

As I got to my car, I vomited. It made me sick to my stomach thinking about all this shit. This motherfucker had been killing everyone, even jurors.

"Shit. I'm marked for death," I said to myself as I drove home.

***

I paced across my living room floor. Taraji had come over to help me with this shit. I knew this motherfucker was going to come to my house and kill me.

"Bitch, you are telling me this motherfucker has hits out on all the people who testified against him?"

"Yeah, bitch, he do. He's killing jurors too. They're finding them dead left and right."

"What are you going to do?"

"I don't know. My head's all fucked up."

"Have you told Keith and your friends?"

"Hell no. Keith knows about the murders. He saw it on the news."

"You should tell them."

"No shit. But I don't know how to do it. I can't just say, 'I was working for the Feds to get you out of jail, now you're all in danger. My bad.' "

"You have to find a way before it's too late."

"I know, you're right."

"What have the Feds offered?"

"Witness Protection program."

"What did you say?"

"Hell fuck no."

"Why not?"

"I just told you. I haven't told Keith."

"Shouldn't you be more concerned about Keith and the kids?"

"Yes, but…"

"But what?"

"I don't know." I sat down next to her.

"Damn, baby girl." She rubbed my back as I lay across her thighs. "I'm here for you."

"I know. I have to face the music. I can't hide from this."

"I can stay with you for a while until you tell him."

"He's out of town."

My phone rang. I answered.

A voice said, "Bitch, you're not safe. I will kill your ass."

"Motherfucker, come on." I slammed the phone on the table.

"Who was that?" Taraji said.

"A motherfucker threatening me." I went to my room and grabbed my .38 from the closet.

"Where did you get the gun?"

"I've had it a while."

"I'm staying here tonight."

"Thanks."

CHAPTER 25
Shantell
One week later

As I walked around the Oakwood mall shopping, I thought I was tripping, because it felt like these two Mexican men were following me. I might be a little paranoid because my mind was still fucked up from what the prosecutor told me about the letter. I still hadn't figured out a way to tell everybody about the situation without them freaking out. Especially Keith. It wouldn't be so bad to tell Keith, but he had told me not to do it, and I went against what he had told me not to do.

As I came out of the Victoria's Secret store, I spotted the two men sitting on the bench looking at me. One had a lot of tattoos on his face with a bald head. The other one had long black hair. They were each wearing blue jeans with a white button down shirt and black boots.

I looked around for the nearest exit trying to get to my car. These motherfuckers looked like they were trying to kidnap me. I'd be damned if I would be laying in the back of a trunk or somewhere in a hole in the desert chopped up. Fuck that.

I walked fast to the nearest exit, heading to my car. They were close behind me. When I made it to my car, my tires were flat.

I looked back at the men coming close to me. My heart was beating out my chest and my hands were sweating. I just knew it was for me.

Just then I saw the parking lot police. I walked over to his car, flagging him down.

"Yes, can I help you?" he asked.

"Yes. I need help. My car tires are flat."

"Okay, I'll call somebody for you."

I looked back at my car and the men following me were gone.

***

I was at Taraji's house. I really needed to talk to someone.

Shit was getting deeper by the minute, and I still hadn't told anyone.

Keith was still in Atlanta trying to get a new contract. We had bought a house there as well. I didn't feel safe in our current house any longer, especially with the kids were there.

When I knocked, Taraji flung open the door with a blunt in her mouth. "Why the fuck you sweating?"

"Bitch, I got chased by two Mexican men."

"What? Where at?"

"At the mall."

"Bitch, come in."

I pulled the blunt from her mouth, hitting it. "Bitch, this shit is real."

"Now tell me what happened."

"Bitch, I was shopping in Oakwood. I thought I was tripping at first, you know. But when I came out the store, they were right there looking at me."

"How they look?"

"One had tattoos on his face and the other one had long black hair."

"So did they chase you?"

"Yeah, bitch. When I made it to my car, that bitch was on four flats."

"How you get away?"

"I flagged down the police in the parking a lot."

"Did you tell the police what was going on?"

"Hell no. I just told him that I needed help with my tires.

"So you still haven't told Keith? Or anyone else?"

"I haven't built up the balls yet."

"Shantell, this shit is getting serious."

"It is serious. Bitch, they're trying to kill me."

"Where are the kids?"

"Spending the night at their grandmother's house. I can't be home by myself."

"Where's Keith?"

"Atlanta. He's bidding for a city contact."

"Are y'all still moving there?"

"Yeah, we just put a down payment on a house."

"Good."

"But I need the rest of this shit behind me."

"I know. You can stay here as long as you want to."

"Thanks. I'm going to need a strong drink and some more weed."

"Just went and copped some."

"Good. I need it bad. I need to take this edge off."

"I feel you."

***

Sandra

Bobby and I sat at the table at Houston's Restaurant in Slidell, having lunch. We had started getting a little bit closer after our first sex encounter.

"So how's the case coming? Y'all getting closer to finding the person that's killing everybody?" I asked.

"Not really. Looks like they are one step ahead of us every time," he said, sipping on his beer.

"What you mean?" I took a bite of my fish.

"Between me and you, I think somebody in the office is giving them the information."

"No, I can't believe that."

"I keep telling you, you're dealing with regular people."

"I been thinking about going to see Deloso."

"For what?"

"To see if I can get him to stop all this killing."

"Good luck with that."

"Why you say that?"

"A man like Deloso don't have a heart. He don't give a fuck about nobody. You don't become the boss of all bosses in Mexico by having a heart. This motherfucker is a cold-blooded killer."

"People change."

"You think? You just helped give him four life sentences."

"You never know."

"Try and see. But enough about that. What you doing later on?"

"Why?" I smiled.

"Well, I was thinking about coming over later."

"Well, I don't have to go back to the office since it's Friday. How about right now?"

As soon as we hit my house door, clothes went to flying everywhere. I ripped my thong off. He picked me up, slammed me against the wall, and thrust his big hard dick in and out of my soaking wet pussy as I held on for dear life. The deeper he went, the more I came all over his dick.

He bent me over the couch, spread my ass cheeks, and slammed his dick in me. I slammed my ass back on him as he gripped my shoulder and pulled my hair, fucking the shit out of me.

"I'm about to cum," he said, shaking.

I slammed my ass back on his dick as he shot his hot come all in my pussy.

CHAPTER 26
Keith

I left city hall after meeting with Atlanta's mayor. One of my partners back in the day knew people. He had moved to Atlanta and had a couple of connects in the government who were close to the mayor. I told him that I was trying to open a construction company in Atlanta.

Shantell and I both wanted to move to Atlanta for a fresh start. I knew I hadn't been spending time with her like I had promised. It was hard to get a business off the ground. It was even harder to restore one to what it once was. Before prison, my company was valued at $50 million. Now, it's not even half that. I had to look ahead. In ten years, I'd be 50. I want to kick back on a tropical island and let my money work for me.

But I got to spend more time with Shantell. I can tell it annoys her when I come home and don't want to fuck. It's not her; it's me. I'm so worn out from working that all I want to do is sleep. That's not good. If I don't drop that dick in her, then somebody else will.

A nigga still can't really believe that I'm free and at home.

I was taking my gray Range Rover back to the hotel. At a light, I was looking at a fine yellow bitch with leggings walking across the street. Out of nowhere, a truck rammed me from behind. I started to get out of my truck when I saw two tattooed Mexican guys who had guns.

I pulled away quickly as they shot at my truck. Looking in my mirror, I saw the truck coming up fast again. I swerved to try to avoid them, but they pulled alongside me. The passenger aimed his gun at me. I swerved to avoid the shot and rammed into the back of a parked car. I saw them drive on as I passed out.

I awoke in a hospital. I had a horrible headache and really didn't know why I was there. I tried to get up, but a nurse held me down.

"You need to rest. You have a bad concussion."

"What happened?"

"You lost control of your truck and hit a parked car."

Then I remembered. I was running from Mexicans who were trying to kill my ass. I didn't even remotely know why. It seemed like more than road rage. It looked personal. The shit looked like a hit.

"Where my phone? I need to call my wife to let her know what happened."

***

Shantell

I was in my bubble bath sipping on Ciroc, snorting a little coke, and hitting some weed. I was all fucked up.

I was so fucking confused about my life. It didn't make any sense. I didn't know if I was coming or going. I was half-assed in love with my husband and dick-whipped by another man I was in love with. I got my family in some bullshit, and the cartel wanted to kill me and all of them plus my friends. I had to tell everyone everything. It was time to face the music. I owed them that.

I snorted another line of coke. I guess a bitch needs to go to rehab as well. I needed to get my mind right. But I needed this shit to get me through this pain and my fucking real life situation.

What kind of bitch am I? I let my kids leave the house knowing they could be killed any time. I was supposed to protect them, not hurt them. My husband was in danger too just because I wanted his black ass out of prison.

My phone rang.

"What's up, girl?" It was Taraji.

"Nothing. I'm in the tub with my head all fucked up."

"What's wrong?"

"You already know. I'm stressing over all this bullshit."

"Let's go to the salon. We can talk about it."

"Give me a half hour."

"Sure."

I got out of the tub and put on a red sundress. It was too hot for panties. Also, I shaved her today. She needed to air out.

About forty-five minutes later, Taraji and I were side by side at the salon getting our nails done.

"I've been thinking of telling everybody," I started.

"Why? Did something else happen?"

"No, but…"

"What?"

"It's hard telling people you love that you put them in danger."

"Bitch, if you leave them hanging, you a piece of shit."

"I know."

"You want me to tell Keith?"

"Bitch, you want Keith to kill you? You must have forgot what kind of nigga you dealing with."

"I feel that too."

"I'm tired of carrying this shit around with me. I need to be free of it. This guilt shit is killing me."

"I feel you."

"Bitch, you don't know how hard it's been. When my kids go to school, I worry they won't come home. If something happened to them, I couldn't forgive myself. I'd kill myself." Tears streamed down my face.

"It'll be all right."

Taraji handed me a tissue to wipe my face. We left the salon. We sat in my car talking. My tears continued to flow.

"It's going to be all right, baby girl," she began.

"Shit, it sure doesn't feel like it."

"I'm here for you. Whatever you need me to do."

"I know, but it's time I face the music."

My phone rang. It was Keith. "Hey, baby," I said. "What's up?"

"I'm in the hospital."

"What? Why?"

"Two Mexicans tried to kill me."

"What?"

"They rammed my truck. They tired shooting at me and chasing me down."

My heart missed a beat. This shit meant those motherfuckers had been following him. "Are you all right?"

"Some bruises. A minor concussion. I'll be home tomorrow."

"Okay. I love you." We hung up.

"What happened?" asked Taraji.

I couldn't talk.

"What's going on? You're scaring me." Taraji turned to me.

"Keith. Keith."

"Keith? What about him?"

"They tried to kill him in Atlanta."

"What? Did he say who?"

"I think it was the same motherfuckers who tried to kill me."

"What the fuck? They're following him?"

"Yes."

"Fuck. You got to tell everybody right now."

CHAPTER 27
Sandra

I walked down a hallway of the parish jail where Deloso was held. The Feds had him in an undisclosed location outside of New Orleans. I came to talk to him and stop his revenge killings. Three more bodies had been discovered this morning. Same old scene: throats cut, two shots in the head. I hadn't heard from Shantell. I hoped she was all right.

I sat in a booth in a red chair. A big piece of bulletproof glass divided us.

Three guards escorted Deloso in. He was wearing a red jumpsuit with red slippers. He was handcuffed with a belly chain and leg shackles. He had gained weight since the trial. His beard had grown out.

"What brings you to see me, counselor?" he asked.

"You know why I'm here."

"More dead bodies?"

"You're an animal. How can you live with yourself?"

"I sleep just fine."

"These people are innocent."

"Are they? They're the reason I got four life sentences."

"That's your doing."

"Whatever. Why are you here?"

"You need to stop the hits."

"Now you want something from me? When I offered earlier, you didn't want to do it."

"I don't know why I came. I thought you might have a heart."

"It was taken from me a long time ago, when I was a child."

"Don't you feel anything?"

"For whom?"

"Anyone."

"If you're not here to talk about releasing me, then we have nothing to talk about."

"Releasing you? Never."

"How's the mayor's race going?"

"You've been following me?"

"I hope you live to see your dream come true."

"Is that threat?"

"Of course not. I just worry for you."

I slammed the phone down and left. I was upset and trying to figure out why I ever came in the first place.

***

Deloso

I paced back and forth in my cell, thinking about what the prosecutor asked me. This bitch had the nerve to come down here and ask me to have mercy on the witnesses and jurors in my case. Fuck them bitches after they gave me four life sentences. Plus she said I don't have a heart. Heart gets you fucked up where I'm from. In Mexico, you can have a heart, but your ass got to be ruthless.

I learned it the hard way at a young age. I was nine when the cartel shot my daddy in the head and raped my mother in front me, all because my father wouldn't join the cartel. See, in Mexico, the cartel runs everything. And if you not down with them, they'll kill your whole family and put poles up their asses and hang them on display for everybody to see. I can't tell you how many times I walked to the store and seen people hanging like that. So if compassion is what that bitch is looking for, it's not here. All them motherfuckers going to die, even her ass.

This black nigga bitch isn't dead yet. She got to be the luckiest bitch in the world. Her and her husband. I sent two of my men to kidnap her and the bitch got away. And I also sent them to kill Keith, and he survived. Right now, I'm going to turn up the heat.

My slot opened and a cell phone came through. I dialed my brother's number.

"Hello," he said.

"Get all this bitch's friends."

"Okay, I'm on it."

"I want you to send this black bitch a message."

"What is it?"

"Tell her 'I'm not to be fucked with. You can run, but you can't hide.' "

"Okay."

"Love you."

"Same here."

I laid back on my bed thinking about this master plain I was putting together to get this bitch. Ain't no way in the world I'm going to do life in the U.S. I needed to be back in Mexico where I was running things.

***

Sandra

I laid my head on Bobby's chest after some much-needed sex. I had been tensed up and stressed out ever since I left from visiting Deloso. In all my years of prosecuting people, I never ran into someone like that. That motherfucker don't have a heart, for real. And he really don't give a fuck.

"So how'd it go with Deloso?"

"Bad."

"I told you."

"I know, but I had to do something. People's lives are in danger."

"Are you scared?"

"Scared of what?"

"Something happening to you?"

"No, not really. If it's my time, it's my time."

"Well, just know this. I'm not going to let nothing happen to you."

"How sweet."

"I'm serious. I love you."

"You love me? Where did that come from?" I raised my head up, looking him in the eyes.

"Don't act surprised."

"I didn't know you cared so much. I thought we were just sexing."

"Well, I can put you back in the friend zone."

"No, I was just playing."

I climbed on top of him and slid his dick in my pussy. I began tongue kissing him too.

"Love you," I said, riding his dick.

***

Brittney

Life had been treating me well. I had opened up my second strip club on the north side of Houston. I moved into a half million dollar house in Katy, Texas and I was driving my dream car, a white Bentley. I even had a new boo. He was tall and black with a big dick and fresh out of prison from doing ten years. He gave me the dick on the regular in every hole.

I ran the money through the money machine, making sure it was all there before I brought it to the bank. I grabbed the money and stuffed it in my bag. I was in a rush to leave because my man was taking me out tonight.

I heard through the streets Eric was dead. Deloso had him killed in prison after he made a deal to testify on him.

I'm glad I got out of all that shit before it went left, but I don't blame Eric for taking a deal. I wouldn't have done life for nobody either, not even my grandmother who raised me because my mother was a hoe who died from an overdose when I was fourteen.

I got a lot of my hoe ways from my mother, running the streets, looking for love in all the wrong places. But I got my shit together, went off to college. I went to moving weight for my ex-boyfriend, who got killed. Then I started stripping and moving weight for different niggas. I got caught by the Feds and did five years. After I got out, I went back to stripping.

I was glad to see that bitch Shantell who helped me get where I'm at now. I've been blessed. Life's good.

Outside my club, two men jumped out of a black van. Both were wearing ski masks. They grabbed me and threw me in the van while I was kicking and screaming. A gun hit the back of my head and everything went black.

I woke up later. My head was hurting, and I was handcuffed to an iron chair in a warehouse. I was surrounded by men speaking Spanish. I understood a little. I'd lived around that my whole life. They were talking about some ratting shit. They mentioned Shantell's name.

I opened my eyes. A bright light was in my face. I couldn't see anything.

"Is your friend's name Shantell?" The speaker was a tall Mexican man with tattoos all over his face and arms.

I slowly spoke. "Yes."

"Was you part of it?"

A million thoughts ran through my head. I wondered if Shantell had stolen money or drugs. If you get in with the cartel, it can be hard to get out. You have to pay your way out. Even then, they might kill you. I hoped this bitch hadn't gotten me into no deep shit with these people. I hadn't talked to her in months. She called me a few months before, but I missed her call. I was living it up in Miami. I hoped these motherfuckers found her. By the look on their faces, that bitch did some serious shit.

"I don't know what y'all talking about?"

I could tell from his expression that it was the wrong answer. My stomach was in a knot. It felt like I was going to shit on myself.

He grabbed my head and turned it to a nearby table. Something was there, but I couldn't tell what. He shined the light on it, and I threw up.

It was Ke'shon. They had cut him up into pieces.

I cried and tried to break free. "Let me go." Help! Help me!"

He grabbed me by the hair. "Shut the fuck up, bitch." He was holding a blood-crusted machete in his hand. "So you don't know what Shantell did?"

I shook my head. I hoped it didn't piss him off. It looked like he wanted to use his machete.

Then a Mexican with long black hair wearing a white suit walked in. "Do you know why I have you here?"

I shook my head. Tears poured down my face. "Please, I don't have nothing to do with this shit."

"See, your nigga friend didn't want to tell me what I need to know. Shantell was working for the Feds as a C.I. She set my brother up. Do you know why?" I shook my head. "She wanted to get her husband out of jail."

I couldn't believe that bitch did this to us. What kind of game was she playing? I was tied up and going to get my head cut off because Keith wanted her to be a C.I. to get him out of jail. I swear if these people let me go, I'd kill this bitch myself.

"Listen, Mister, I don't know anything about this ratting shit, but if you let me go, I'll find her for you. Please don't kill me."

"I'm going to let you go, but I need you to give her a message."

Thank you, Jesus. "Anything you want me to do, I will do."

"I know you will. Tell her Deloso says she's dead." He spoke to the other guys in Spanish, and they beat me. They hit me in the face, stomach, and everywhere. They broke my jaw, ribs, nose, and more. I stated vomiting blood. I thought they were going to beat me to death.

I blacked out.

I woke up in the middle of the street in front of my club. I was in agony. I couldn't move. A car stopped just before it hit me. The man rushed from his car to me and called 911.

CHAPTER 28
Shantell

I had spent the night at Taraji's house after we got fucked up by smoking weed and drinking. We spent a lot of time talking about my problems. My phone rang continuously, but I ignored it. I knew it had to be the prosecutor. Two more jurors had been found dead in their homes, double-tapped execution style. They wanted me to go into witness protection. I didn't want to talk to them, but I knew if I didn't, they'd send someone over to talk to me. I didn't need no more added stress on my plate. I had prayed about this whole situation. I put God on my heart to make me tell everyone involved. I was being selfish. A lot of other lives were at risk.

I had been trying to call Brittney's ass. I was going to tell her first. She'd take it better than the others. But the hoe wasn't answering her phone.

I had a different plan for Keith. I was going to make his favorite meal and then suck and fuck him real good. Then I'd tell him. Or perhaps, even better, I could go to Darrell's condo in Houston and call and tell Keith from there. That way he couldn't beat or kill my ass. By the time he found out where I called from, I could be in a new home in a new country.

I knew Jackie was mad at me, but only because I kept her out of the loop. She was the one who gave me the game on how to do this shit.

As I walked in the house, my phone rang. I didn't recognize the number, but knew it had to be the Feds. I had enough. I answered the phone with an attitude. "What the fuck you—"

A woman's soft voice began. "May I speak to Ms. Shantell Washington?"

"This her." I sounded confused.

"I'm Emily Simpson. I'm a nurse at Ben Taub Hospital in Houston."

"Hospital?

"Yes, ma'am."

"Is everything okay? What's going on?"

"Do you know Brittney Fork?"

"Yeah. Is she all right?"

"No. She was found beaten really badly in the street. She's lost a lot of blood."

"I'll get there as soon as I can."

I got a flight out that afternoon. I was at the hospital and running up to a nurse's station in just a few hours.

"What room is Brittney Fork in?"

"Your name?"

"Shantell Washington."

"She's in 218."

As I walked to the room, a chill ran through my body.

She was lying there with tubes and wires everywhere. She was covered in bandages from head to toe. Crying, I grabbed her hand. It was my fault she was fucked up and in the hospital.

The nurse said it wouldn't be long. There was a serious hemorrhage. Too much swelling in the brain. She had been beaten so badly that I couldn't even recognize her.

Her eyes opened slowly.

"Hey baby." I smiled.

She tried to talk, but I couldn't hear her. Her voice was broken like everything else. I got closer.

She whispered, "You should have told me that you were working for the Feds."

"I'm sorry. Please, forgive me. Please." My tears flowed freely.

"Deloso's brother wanted me to send you a message."

"What?"

She took a halting breath and uttered, "He's going to kill everything you love." Her eyes closed. She lay back, seemed to fight for her breath. Then nothing.

The heart monitor flat lined. Bells and alarms were everywhere.

"Brittney! Brittney! No. Please. God help her." I hugged her tightly as doctors and nurses flooded the room.

I was rushed back as they made a frantic effort to revive her.

But there was no use. She was gone. I told the hospital to send me the bill. Then I flew home.

Keith met me at the door. "I'm sorry, baby. I know how close y'all were. Anything you need me to do?"

"Not right now. I'm about to take a hot bath."

I got in the tub. I felt bad for a lot of reasons. I had lied to Keith. I said Brittney was in a car wreck. But I got Brittney murdered. Maybe if I committed suicide, all this shit would go away. Then Keith and the kids would be safe.

I snorted a line of coke and hit the weed. As I started to let myself slide beneath the water, my phone rang and Icy came running into my bathroom, crying loudly.

"What's wrong?" I asked.

"Jac—Jac— Jackie's dead. "

"What?"

"It's on the news."

I looked at my phone. A text was waiting. It read, "Ur next."

I rushed out of the bathroom and it was on CNN news. I saw Jackie getting in her truck at her salon. It exploded as she cranked it.

"And that's not all. Police found Ke'shon's body on the Northside of Houston," Icy said.

I dropped my phone and ran to the bathroom, throwing up in the toilet. I had gotten my friends killed over a bunch of bullshit. These motherfuckers were not playing fair. My husband and kids could be next. Maybe I should turn myself over to Deloso's brother so that no one else had to die.

I balled up on the bathroom floor and cried my soul out. Icy fruitlessly to console me.

Deloso was behind this. He wanted to send me a message loud and clear.

Icy helped me up off the floor. My legs felt like overcooked spaghetti. She helped me to the bedroom. She lay next to me, rubbing my back. It felt like my heart and soul had been ripped out of me. "It's all my fault."

"Don't say that."

"It is. Is Keith gone?"

"He was leaving when I got here."

"So he don't know about Jackie."

"No. What's going on? Why is it your fault?"

I got up and paced back and forth across the room.

"What's going on?" There was a catch in her voice. She sat on the bed Indian style. I stared at her wordlessly. "Talk to me, Shantell."

I grabbed my coke from the closet and poured a large amount on the dresser. I quickly snorted two lines.

Icy got out of bed and walked over to me as I did another line. "What's wrong with you, Shantell?"

I looked at her, then turned down to snort another line. She grabbed it and threw it in the trash can.

"Bitch, is you crazy? That was a thousand dollar's worth of shit!" I cried.

"So?"

"Look, you need to go."

"I ain't going anywhere until you talk to me and tell me what the fuck is going on."

"Get the fuck out of my house!" I screamed.

"I'm not going anywhere."

I went to her. I tried to slap her, but she pushed me back onto the bed and straddled my body, pinning arms down."

"Get off me. Get the fuck off me." I struggled, but she was stronger than me.

"No."

I tried to move her. I kicked and screamed. But she wasn't going anywhere. I broke down in tears.

She bent in and tongue kissed me. I gave in and kissed her back. She went down on me, eating my pussy. I grinded my pussy in her face, cumming back to back.

Icy abruptly got up and put on her shoes.

"Where are you going? I asked.

"I don't have time for this shit. I'm out."

"Please don't go."

She walked downstairs and to the door.

I couldn't let her leave. She was one of the few friends I had left. I couldn't lose her over bullshit. If I let her leave, I might never see her again. I had to warn her. I owed her so much more than that.

I grabbed her arm. "Don't leave."

"Why shouldn't I?"

"I have to tell you something."

"I'm listening." She looked dead serious and had her hands on her hips.

"Jackie, Ke'shon, and Brittney are dead and it's my fault. I was working for the Feds to get Keith out of jail."

"What? When?"

"Come into the living room. I'll explain." I lit a blunt hit and passed it to her. "They gave Keith thirty years when he wouldn't tell on the cartel. I went behind his back and made a deal with the Feds to gets him out. Jackie gave me the idea."

"Wait, Jackie knew about this?"

"No."

"Does Keith know?"

"No. He told me not to do it. He knew all this shit would happen."

"What does Keith think is going on?"

"I told him Brittney died in a car accident."

"When will you tell him?"

"I'm not."

"You're not?"

"You know what he'll do to me if he finds out?"

"He might not have a chance, the way this guy is moving."

"I'm going back to the Feds. They said they could protect us."

"Damn, Shantell. You are a bitch for this. You should have been told us."

"I'm sorry."

"You're fucking right you're sorry. You put everyone in danger, and you weren't even going to tell us."

"I know." I grabbed her hand. "Please forgive me."

"You need to figure this shit out. You need to tell Keith, or I will."

***

Icy

I jumped in my car and pulled off .38 hot. I couldn't believe this bitch got everybody involved in her shit, especially with the motherfucking cartel, of all people. This bitch been working for the Feds all this time. And the cold part about it is that the hoe didn't even tell us. That's crazy! It would be one thing if we all was in it together, but it's a whole other thing being selfish. Your own husband don't know? This a man you say you love. It wouldn't surprise if the cartel thinks Keith put her up to do it. Crazy part is, Keith is a real good guy. He would give her the world.

I wish I could find a nigga like Keith. Fine, big dick, and loving. Hoes like Shantell always get the good man and fuck them over.

My thoughts were interrupted by my phone ringing.

"Hello?"

"What's up, you still trying to get this?"

"Yes."

"Okay, meet me at the spot."

"Okay, I'm on my way."

I pulled up to the Walmart parking lot. I jumped in James's black BMW. James was brown-skinned and cute, but he was gay. He worked at the post office. That's where he gets the check from. What he was doing now was busting government checks. A bitch got to eat. He's the one that put me in the game. We go back to high school.

"What's wrong with you, girlfriend. Man troubles?"

"No, nothing like that.

"Attitude!"

"You got the stuff or what?"

"Here you go."

"Here's the two racks."

"Okay."

"I'm out."

"Bye, bitch."

I jumped in my car, pulling off.

***

Shantell

What have I done? I needed a break. I needed to get away and get out of the city for a minute. I got in my truck and pulled off.

About four hours later, I pulled up to Darrell's condo.

I know I didn't need to be here and I said I was done with him, but I needed to clear my head.

I stepped out of my truck, walking up to his condo. I know he was there because I saw his car. Everything in me was telling me this was a bad idea, but I didn't listen to my gut. Instead, I listened to my pussy. I walked up to his door and knocked on it. I was nervous as hell. I hadn't talked to or seen him in months. I wanted to turn and walk away, but it was too late.

As I was about to walk off, the door opened and he was standing in some white boxer brief with nothing else on. My thoughts immediately left me.

***

Darrell

I couldn't believe she was here at my front door. She looked so good with her tight blue jeans on and her hair hanging long. I wasn't even going to ask her why she was here. I didn't care.

I pulled her into the house and tongue kissed her. She didn't even stop me. I picked her up, carrying her to the bedroom. I laid her on the bed and pulled her panties and jeans off at the sometime. I went down on her, sucking her fat pearl tongue.

"Yes, baby, don't stop." She grabbed my head.

I sucked on her pearl tongue as she shook out of control,

cumming all in my mouth. I put her legs on my shoulder and slid my dick into her soaking wet pussy. I thrust harder and deeper into her as she dug her nails into my back and bit me on the neck.

"Don't stop. Give me that dick."

I flipped her over in a doggy style position and spread her cheeks, sticking my finger in her asshole and slamming my dick in and out of her pussy as she moaned, gripping the sheets. She slammed back on me as we went at it. I began to shake, gripping her ass cheeks real tight.

"I'm cumming. I'm cumming." She pushed her ass harder on me as I shot all my nut into her. We fell on the bed, not saying a word, trying to catch our breaths.

She laid on my chest as I put my arms around her. I felt tears falling on my chest.

CHAPTER 29
Shantell

Two weeks later, I held a funeral for Jackie, Ke'shon, and Brittney. Keith held me as I cried. The minister droned on about how death was a beginning of a journey, not an end. As he prayed and said a final amen, Keith hugged me and then left to go back to work.

I got in my car and drove around aimlessly. I found myself in front of the Federal Building. All my friends were dead. It was all my fault. The witness protection program didn't seem like a bad thing anymore. I wandered zombie-like to the prosecutor's office. I needed to talk to Sandra Lewis.

I walked in her office, and she looked up at me. "Have a seat."

"This motherfucka has killed my friends. I think my family is next."

"I've been trying to tell you this."

"I need your help for real now."

"We'll get you into witness protection. We'll provide you and your family with new identities in a new state."

"What about my other friend? She part of this too."

"You need to tell them to come see me."

"I need a little time to tell my husband."

"I can help you with that if needed."

"I need to be the one that tells him and the kids."

"Remember, this is urgent. Get back here as quick as you can."

"Okay."

I left the building. I was headed to my mother's house to get the kids. I tried calling my mother and kids, but got no answer.

***

Keith

Everything was great. My construction company was going

good. I was about to get a big city contract to build a new $20 million hospital. Baldwin was on his way. I was going to have him help me with the paperwork to open up in Atlanta.

My secretary called and told me Baldwin was here and sent him into my office.

"Glad you could make some time for me," I said, shaking his hand.

"You're my partner. I always have time for you."

"Have a seat. And thank you for the check."

"It's all good. So what's up?"

"I'm trying to open an office in Atlanta."

"Shouldn't be a problem."

"We should sign the contact for the hospital soon."

"That should help."

"I'm back. Life is good."

"I'm happy for you. Hey, I got to get to a meeting."

"I'll walk you out."

We walked outside together. He got in and started his car. It exploded and threw me to the ground.

"What the fuck?" I tried to get off the ground, but I was dazed and shaking my head. "Call 911!" I screamed.

I watched as his body burned in the car.

Why would someone kill my lawyer? Unless somebody was trying to send me a message.

The police and a fire truck got there and tried to put out the fire. A police officer came ova to me. "What happened?"

"I really don't know. He started his car, and it blew up."

"Do you know if anyone had been threatening him?"

"No."

"If you find out anything, call me." He handed me a card. Do you need me to call you an ambulance?"

"I'm fine."

"Thank you, sir."

I went back to my office. My head hurt, and I still felt fucked up. I couldn't believe Baldwin was dead. I looked at my phone on my desk. Shantell had called me twice. I dialed her number.

***

Shantell

When nobody answered at my mother's house, I rushed over. I jumped out of my car almost before it stopped and ran to the front door. It was open. I took out my .38 - I carry it everywhere now - and slowly walked in. I was scared to death, but I wasn't going out without a fight.

I called for my mother and the kids, but no one answered. My stomach felt like it was tied in a knot. I yelled hers and the kids' names again and again as I ran from room to room.

I found my mother in the kitchen. She had been shot twice in the back of the head, and her throat was cut. I dropped to my knees beside her body. Tears flowed freely.

"Mom, Mom. No, I'm sorry! I swear I'm sorry! It should have been me!" I screamed.

I saw a black box on the kitchen table. I opened it. There was a cell phone. I turned it on. I saw my worst nightmare come to life. My kids were tied up naked. Tape covered their mouths. They were crying. I pushed the play button.

A Mexican man who was bald with tattoos everywhere was holding a gun to Keith Jr.'s head. He said, "You black bitch. You think you can cross my boss and get away with it? If you want to get your kids back, you have to make a decision."

Then another man with long black hair that looked like Deloso went to talking. "I'll trade their lives for yours, or you can give your husband up. Whichever you want."

I threw the phone on the ground. I ran out to my car. My head was all fucked up.

My phone rang. I answered. It was Keith.

"Somebody just killed Baldwin," Keith said.

"What?"

"His car blew up. Right in front of me."

"We have bigger problems."

"What are you talking about?"

"I'll come to your office. Give me ten minutes."

"What the fuck is going on?"

"I'm going to tell you."

"Meet me at the house."

"Okay."

I had to come up with a lie. Not no bullshit either. It had to sound good. If this nigga found out what I'd done, he was going to kill my ass. I needed to find out if the Feds would help me get my kids back.

When I got to the house, his car was already there. I ran through the story in my head. Don't get it twisted. I was hurting for my kids, but I needed to buy time.

I ran into the house crying. I hugged Keith tight. I needed him to feel guilty.

"What's going on?" He was holding me tight.

I mumbled incoherently.

"What?"

"Somebody killed my mother."

"What? When?"

"I don't know. I went to her house. She was dead."

"What?"

"And our kids are gone."

"Somebody kidnaped our kids? Fuck!" He paced back and forth. He flipped over a glass table. It's shattered and glass flew everywhere. He knocked everything down on the TV.

"Baby, calm down."

"What the fuck you mean calm down? Some motherfucker kidnaped my kids."

"They're mine too. Maybe it's something you did?"

"What, bitch? Are you saying it's my fault?" He looked like he wanted to kill me.

"It might be some old beef from when you were on the streets."

He didn't answer. He stormed through the door. I came up behind him screaming his name. I hoped the nigga didn't find out anything.

I called the prosecutor, but I didn't get an answer. "Fuck, where's this bitch when I need her?" I said to myself. "Fuck this." I got my gun from my purse. I sat on my bed. I put the gun in mouth. If I was dead, all this went away. I cocked the hammer back. My finger was tight on the trigger. Tears rolled down my face.

I looked at a picture of my family on the nightstand. I thought about Keith and the kids. I couldn't do it. It wouldn't get my kids out of trouble.

I grabbed the picture off the nightstand and broke down crying. I thought about them being naked and afraid, calling for their daddy and mother to help them.

I fell back, balling up in the middle of bed, hoping I would die as I cried myself to sleep.

I really had fucked up this time.

Robert Baptiste

CHAPTER 30
Keith

I drove around the city for hours. My head was smoking, and I was crying. I thought about my kids. I imagined then crying out for me. My past had come back to haunt me and even worse, everyone I loved was in the middle of my shit. How in the fuck did I let this happen? I should have never left the streets. These motherfuckers know if I was still in the streets, they wouldn't have tried me like this. When a nigga tries to change his life and takes his foot off these niggas' necks who still in the streets, they think a nigga went soft. But these niggas about to see me act a motherfucking fool.

And to kill my mother-in-law? They must have thought she was holding money and drugs for me. It must be a young, dumb-ass nigga to fuck with me like this. I swear whoever did this will pay with their lives. And their family's lives. That's on my mother's grave.

I was surprised that I hadn't received a call for money. I needed to hit up a few O.G. niggas that were still in the streets. I thought about my nigga Brad. He was still in the game. I think he might know something to help me.

I called him. He answered on the first ring. "What's up, nigga?" I asked.

"Man, you don't sound right."

"I'm fucked up."

"What are you talking about?"

"Man, somebody kidnapped my kids."

"What? When?"

"Today. Someone ran into my mother-in-law's house, killed her, and took my kids. I need your help."

"Man, I ain't got time for games."

"I ain't playing."

A video downloaded. I pressed play on my phone. I saw my kids naked and tied up. I saw a bald Mexican with tattoos holding a gun to them, and a Mexican man dressed in a white suit talking.

"What's this shit?" I asked.

"Listen to it."

The words chilled me. "You black bitch. The only way you get your kids back is if you trade your life for theirs."

"This motherfucker? I don't owe that nigga shit. I stopped messing with him years ago. Who is he talking about?" I asked.

"You don't recognize him? Look close."

"Shit. What the fuck?"

"That's Deloso's brother and his worker."

"Man, what the fuck is he doing with my kids? What the fuck is going on around here?"

"Your wife owes him."

"My wife? What does she have to do with this?"

"Everything."

"She doesn't even know Deloso."

"Maybe you don't know your wife."

"Man, stop talking in riddles. Spit it out."

"I'll show you."

He sent me another video. I started watching it. I saw my wife with millions of dollars in front of her. Jackie, Brittney, Ke'shon, and Kesha were all there. They were talking shit about how much money they were getting. What fucked me up more is that they were standing in front of a lot of bricks

"I need a minute. I'll get back with you," he said, hanging up.

I pulled up to a church and sat outside of it and prayed. "Look, God, I know I ain't been the best person in the world. I've done some fucked-up shit to people and their families. Please don't let my sins fall on my kids. Please, God. I'm sorry. Please bring my kids back to me, please."

Brad called me back. "Where you at?"

"Parked at a church. Why?"

"Meet me at Church's on M.L.K."

"What for?"

"I know why they took your kids and killed your mother-in-law."

"Alright." I hoped he really knew for sure what was going on.

A few minutes later, Brad pulled up behind me in a black Jeep and walked over to my car.

"What's going on?" I asked.

"Man, it's bad. You saw the videos."

"Nigga, don't fuck with me right now. What was that bullshit? Why the fuck were they in front of bricks of cocaine?"

"Well, your wife went by the name Ms. Bitch and that was her crew."

"Crew?"

"Yeah. They were working for Deloso."

"Why would she do that?"

"To get you out of prison."

"Get me out of prison? Are you serious?"

"This is why he kidnapped your kids."

This shit hit me like a ton of bricks. "She ratted on him?"

"Now you know."

Rage overtook me and I saw nothing but black. This bitch been lying to me the whole time.

"You got your gun on you?"

"What you going to do?"

"Man, give me your gun." I was hot as fish grease. I was going to kill that bitch. She knew what was going on. The bitch played me about my kids. I was going to put a bullet in her head.

***

Shantell

I forced myself out of bed to get something to drink. My head was spinning. I felt bad. The police had called and said they found my mother's body. I needed to go down to identify it.

As I started boiling water, the front door slammed open. Before I could move, I got slapped in the face so hard that I fell on my ass, dazed. Blood was running down my face. When I came to my senses, I was looking down the barrel of a gun.

Keith's eyes were blood red. He had a cold look on his face. His eyes read death. I had never seen this person before. This was motherfucker the streets were afraid of. I knew if I wanted to live, I had better answer any and all the questions. My lying had caught up with me. I thought I could hold out until I could piece shit together. I was hoping that he wouldn't have to find out.

"Bitch, I have some questions. I swear on your kids' lives that if you don't answer straight, I'll put a hole in your head. I won't even give a fuck about it."

I was so scared that it didn't make sense. I felt some piss run down my legs and thought I was going to shit myself. My mouth was trembling. Tears flooded down my face. I was sitting on the floor wearing only a T-shirt.

I had been dreading this day. The shit had finally hit the fan.

Keith raged, "You can wipe away those fucking tears. I don't give a fuck about them. That don't mean shit to me. You had me thinking it was my fault, but it's all your fault. Now tell me everything your bitch ass has been doing since I went to prison. You better not skip a beat or leave anything out."

I stuttered at first. I was scared to death. "I-I-I I w-w-w—"

"What the fuck you saying? Don't fuck with me." I put my hands up in surrender. I looked at him with tears running down my face. "Spit the shit out, bitch."

"I was selling drugs."

"For who?"

"Deloso."

"Why?"

"Because I wanted you home. I wanted our family back together. Our kids needed you. I needed you."

"Do you know what you've done?"

"I'm sorry!"

"Fuck, Shantell. I told you this fucking shit was going to happen."

"I swear it wasn't supposed to turn out like this."

"What the fuck did you think would happen when you told on the cartel?"

"I didn't know."

"Why did you let me believe it was my fault?"

"I couldn't tell you it was mine. I knew how you would act."
"What now?"
"I got to give them what they want."
"What's that?"
"Me."
"I know. I saw the video with Deloso's brother and our kids."
"I'm sorry. I swear I'm sorry." I grabbed his legs.
He pressed the gun to my head.
 I looked at him. "Go ahead. Pull the trigger. I deserve it.
Take me from this misery.

Robert Baptiste

CHAPTER 31
Keith

As much as I wanted to kill her, I couldn't. She was my wife. She was the mother of our kids. Moreover, she did it for me and the kids. It was hard to knock her for that. It was partly my fault. My past had come back to haunt me once again. It took me away from the kids and her.

I looked at her. She was terrified. She was shaking and pissing on herself. Tears and blood flowed down her face. My heart hurt for her. Tears came to my eyes. I knelt down and held her close.

"I'm sorry, baby," she said as she held me tight and sobbed.

"It'll all be all right." I picked her up and carried her to the bathroom. I put her in the tub and gently washed her body. Afterward, I carried her to the bed and made love to her like she was the last women on earth. I held her until she fell asleep.

But I couldn't sleep. My kids were too much on my mind. I thought about killing both Shantell and myself. I figured the kids were dead by now. But that wouldn't bring them back.

I needed to come up with a plan. I went to the backyard to think. I knew this shit would never end because that motherfucker Deloso thought I made Shantell set him up. I see now why them Mexicans was trying to kill me in Atlanta. It doesn't matter what I do. He'll never change his mind. I told her not to fuck with this shit. I knew this would happen. And everyone is dead: her mother, her friends, Baldwin, and likely our kids.

I heard the patio door slide open. Shantell was there wearing a see-through teddy.

"Can I join you?" she asked.

I just looked at her and turned my head. She came over to sit next to me. I was still .38 hot with her. I told her ass not to fuck with this shit. I took a puff from the cigarette and blew the smoke out.

"Can I have a hit?"

I handed it to her and she took a hard pull of the cigarette. I didn't even know she smoked. I guess I really didn't know her.

"When did you start smoking?

"A couple of years back."

"I guess I really don't know shit about you."

"I'm the same person you fell in love with."

"Are you?"

"Do you know how it feels to have your husband - who you love more than life - itself – sent to prison for thirty years?"

"I made the shit. I had to deal with it. I told you not to fuck with this."

"What could I do? Sit around with my thumb in my ass?"

"Do you realize what you did?" She stayed silent. "This shit not a game."

"I know. My mother and best friends are dead. My kids are kidnapped."

"Fuck! I told your ass—"

"It's done now. I'll give myself to the cartel to get our kids back."

"What? Are you tripping? You know what they going to do to you?"

"It's the only way. We going to get our kids back."

"I can't let you do that."

"I have to face the music. Our kids don't deserve this."

"Or we can ask the Feds to help."

"Shantell, listen to what you are saying."

"Everything's my fault."

"I can't let you do it. If anything, I'll go. They think it was me anyway."

"That's sweet. You told me not to, but I did anyway. Let me do this." She got up.

I grabbed her arm and looked deeply into her eyes." I love you."

"I love you too."

"You need to listen to me then."

"Just take good care of the kids. I'm going to talk to the Feds tomorrow."

Now, I was going to lose my wife too. Fuck.

Robert Baptiste

CHAPTER 32
Shantell

Keith and I were in Sandra's office describing the situation with our kids. I told her that the cartel wanted to trade them for me.

"Are you sure you want to do this?" she asked.

"Yes."

"Think carefully about it. It will mean your life."

"The kids don't deserve this."

"We'll help. We want Hernandez Deloso too. That's his brother."

"What do I need to do?"

"We'll put a GPS on you. We can follow where they take you. But this will be dangerous. We can't make any guarantees as to your safety."

"I know. But I'll do whatever it takes to protect my kids."

"Are you okay with this, Mr. Washington?"

"I tried to talk her out of it, but she won't back down. If we get our kids, I'll accept it."

"We'll put together a team and get with you as soon as we can."

"We don't have long. They sent me a video of my kids stripped and tied up."

"We'll do whatever we can for them."

"Thank you."

***

When we got home, Keith and I made love like we were the last people on earth. Then I laid my head on his chest, sobbing.

"You don't have to do this, Shantell."

"Keith, it's all my fault."

"It's my fault too. I shouldn't have forced you into that situation."

"Maybe, but I should have listened to you. I didn't know anything else."

I climbed on top of him and began riding his dick.

Later, I awoke in the middle of the night and went outside. I thought about my kids being scared. Back in the living room, I cried when I looked at their pictures. I picked one up and held it tight against my chest as I cried my heart out.

CHAPTER 33
Shantell

A week later, I was in a van. The Feds were giving me instructions. Yes, the Feds was going to help me get my kids back, but the whole thing was that they wanted Deloso's brother even if the cartel gave me the kids back. They weren't going to move unless they saw him. That's how the Feds work. They were not going to blow their case. They don't care about the cost. It was all about their case. Basically my kids and I are guinea pigs for them.

"Listen, this is a watch which acts like a GPS tracker. It's to help us find you if something happens to you. Now we are not going to move in until we see Hernandez. So that means even if we get your kids, if Hernandez is not with them, we are going to let them take you and bring you to him. So let them do it, and then we are going to find you," Agent Smith said.

I put on a big fake smile, but I was too scared to talk. Keith was in the other van. He didn't want me to do it. He'd tried to talk me out of it again, but I told him it was something I had to do.

I pulled up to this abandoned warehouse like the cartel asked me to. The Feds were in a couple vans down from the warehouse, waiting to make a move once they saw Hernandez. I asked them not to make a move until my kids were safe.

An undercover agent and I stepped out of the car. A few seconds later, a black van pulled up in front of the warehouse. The door opened and two Mexican men got out with shotguns. There were no signs of Hernandez anywhere.

"Get in the van," they ordered.

"Let my kids go first," I replied

"Get in the fucking van!"

"Not until I see my kids."

One of the Mexican pulled my kids from the van. I wanted to break down and cry. They were only wearing their underclothes and their hands were tied up.

"Let them go."

They untied them. They ran over to me. I hugged and kissed

them. "Now go with this nice man." I tried to sound as normal as possible.

"We want to stay with you!" they cried.

"No, go with him, and your daddy is waiting on y'all. Now go."

I watched as the agent placed them in the car.

I walked over to the Mexicans. They grabbed my arms hard, throwing me in the van. The watch broke and fell to the ground. They threw a black hood over my head. I knew I was going to meet Deloso's brother. I was just praying the Feds found me before they killed me.

Whap! They hit me in the back of my head and I went out.

CHAPTER 34
Keith

I was pacing back and forth outside the van. I was happy to see my kids, but now these motherfuckers got my wife. Agent Smith stepped out of the van, trying to explaining this shit to me.

"Where the fuck is my wife?"

"We don't know. We lost her."

"How can y'all let this shit happen? Why the fuck you didn't move in when the motherfuckers gave y'all my kids back?"

"Well, we found her watch on the ground. It must have broken off when they threw her in the van. And besides that, the plan was to get Hernandez."

"So fuck my wife? My kids and wife were y'all's fucking guinea pigs?"

"I'm sorry, but this is how these things work," he stated, emotionless.

Before I knew it, I punched him in the face. Other agents ran over and grabbed me. "Calm down, Mr. Washington," one of them said.

"Get off me!" I pulled away. "You motherfuckers better hope y'all find her or y'all going to see the real Keith."

"Mr. Washington. Let me talk to you."

"About what?"

"Please don't do anything crazy. Let us handle this," the white baldheaded one said.

"Look, this is my wife. If anything happens to her, I'm going to blame you, motherfucker," I said, walking off, getting in my car, and pulling off. I rode around the city, thinking to myself what my next move would be.

***

Shantell

Later, I awoke to someone slapping my face. When I woke up, I wish I hadn't. Deloso's brother and a few of his men surrounded me. They all had whips in their hands. I was butt-naked, hanging from the ceiling of a warehouse. I knew what was coming. I asked God to be ready for my soul. I knew my ass belonged to the cartel. I was ready to face the music.

"You black nigga bitch. You thought you could tell on my brother and get away with it? It doesn't work like that. It's time to pay the piper. Your bitch-ass husband is next."

I wanted to tell him Keith was innocent, but my mouth was taped.

"Whip this bitch. I want the skin to come off this black bitch's ass." He smoked on his cigar, watching.

I felt the whips bite into my body. It felt like my skin was being flayed off. They hit me everywhere: legs, ass, back, breasts, and face. They had no mercy. I moaned and tried to scream as blood flew everywhere. Every time I lost consciousness, a blow to the face would wake me up. I couldn't take it anymore.

I prayed this motherfucker would kill me and just get it over with.

The pain was too great. I passed out.

***

Keith

I couldn't sit back and let them kill Shantell. I knew how these motherfuckers played. I'd never see her again. I did what any boss would do. I got Brad to kidnap Deloso's wife and children. I had told this motherfucker not to cross me. I had reach too. I knew where his family stayed in Texas. That's how close I was to him. He must forgot who I am. I knew how to play this game too.

I had his wife and kids tied up in the warehouse district. This had been my plan from the jump. I went along with Shantell's shit because I couldn't talk her out of it.

I sent Hernandez the same message he sent me. He knew me well. We were a lot alike. Neither of us played fair. Brad was at the warehouse waiting for me to give the word to kill his whole family if this shit went sideways. I picked up the phone, calling this motherfucker. I might been out of the game for a minute, but I still know how to reach motherfuckers when need be.

"Hello," he answered.

"Listen, you wetback nasty motherfucker. Tell your brother I got his family tied up and waiting to be killed. You know me. I don't play no games. If my wife is not alive, he can kiss his family goodbye."

I hung up before he could say anything. I was just waiting for him to call me back, which I knew he would once he got the call from Deloso. He knew I wasn't playing.

***

Hernandez

"Brother, we have a problem."

"I thought you took care of all our problems by now."

"I was. But this motherfucker Keith kidnapped your wife and kids from Houston."

"How in the fuck you let that happen!" he raged.

"I'm sorry."

"What he want?"

"His wife back."

"Where is she?"

"Tied up in the warehouse getting beaten."

"Fuck! Fuck! Take her down now. Get my family back and kill them motherfuckers when you make the trade."

"Okay, I'm on it."

***

Keith

"Hello?"

"Meet me at the warehouse in Texas. You know the spot."

"I'm on my way." I hit Brad up and let him know what the play was.

"My nigga, I'm in this shit with you. I'm going to help you get your wife back," he said once I explained the situation.

"Okay, then we off to Texas."

I had told the Feds about the meeting. They had the place surrounded. I stepped out of the van.

"Let me see my family!" Hernandez shouted.

"Let me see my wife!" I shouted back.

They opened the van. My wife was tied up and bloody. I wanted to start shooting at these motherfuckers. I had made up in my mind I was going to kill Hernandez.

"Now it's your turn," said Hernandez.

Brad slid open the van door, showing him his family.

"Let them go," Hernandez demanded.

"You first." I didn't trust him.

"At the same time."

They untied Shantell while Brad untied Hernandez's family. Shantell looked so weak that she could barely move. They had beaten her. One of his man walked her toward me.

We let his family go. I shot the guy holding my wife in the head. I grabbed her and pulled her down as gunfire erupted. The Feds rushed in, exchanging gunfire. I saw Hernandez trying to run, so I gave chase. He had to pay for what he did to my family.

He spun around and fired two quick shots. On missed. The other hit me in the leg. I buckled and fell.

He walked over and stood over me. His gun was in my face. "You shouldn't have crossed our family. You and that rat bitch of yours is dead." I heard a gunshot and flinched. I thought I was dead.

When I opened my eyes, Shantell was there with a gun in her hand. Deloso's brother had a bullet in his head. She knelt down and hugged and kissed me.

"You killed his ass. I love you." I smiled up at her.

"I told you I'm your ride or die bitch." She smiled back at me.

***

Shantell

A week later, Keith was getting ready to get out the hospital. I had stayed with him every day while he was in there. He was still mad at me for the bullshit I put our family through. I couldn't blame him. I should have listened. My head was all over the place. The Feds were talking about indicting me for murder for killing Hernandez.

"What you thinking about?" Keith asked

"All this drama I put our family through." Tears rolled down my face.

Keith limped over to me and hugged me. "It's okay. The kids are fine now."

"I should have listened. I'm sorry."

"Well, I'm just happy everybody is okay," he said.

"Me too. Damn! I fucked up."

"You did," he agreed.

"So, do you think they going to charge me with murder?"

"I don't know, these bitches play the game raw."

"But I did everything they asked me to do. I swear if we get out of this, I'm done with all this shit and I'm moving the fuck out of New Orleans."

"Sounds good to me." He kissed me. "Love you," he said.

"Love you back."

Just then Sandra and Agent Smith walked into the room.

"We need to talk," Sandra said.

"About what?" I asked like I didn't know.

"You killing Hernandez."

"He was going to kill my husband."

"Well, we really wanted to try him in the courtroom. He killed a federal judge. But we had granted you immunity for all associated crimes in this matter, so we can't charge you. But remember, we don't like vigilantes. If you kill anybody else, your ass will be prosecuted," she said. "Oh, and the charges of assaulting an agent have been dropped against you, Mr. Keith."

They walked out and we both breathed a sigh of relief. Keith and I could start our new life without drama. We could raise our new baby without having to deal with all this shit.

Robert Baptiste

CHAPTER 35
Deloso

I was laying on my bunk in a cell. When the slot popped open. A cell phone and newspaper were handed through. When I saw the front page, my stomach tightened. A rage came over me. I saw my brother's body, a bullet hole in his head. He was surrounded by federal law enforcement officers. I couldn't believe these motherfuckers killed my brother.

I called my personal assassin. I knew he would get the job done, no ifs, ands, or buts about it.

"What do you need, boss?"

"I need you to handle some business. You see what they did to my brother?"

"Yes, sir."

"Take care of everyone like you took care of Dave Green."

"Got it."

"I want everyone dead. Down to the pets.

"I got you. It'll be handled."

"It's worth five million."

I couldn't believe those motherfuckers had killed my brother and put me into prison. They think this is over. It never will be. I'll be out of this motherfucker real soon. Then it's gonna get real. They can't keep me down.

***

Sandra

I stood at the podium outside the federal building with Bobby, Frank, and the mayor standing beside me while the camera flashed from the reporters.

I was glad that they had killed Deloso's brother because if not, we were going to have to cut him loose so the killing would stop.

I heard Shantell and her family made it out safe. That's good. Maybe next time she'll listen to me.

I cleared my throat and started talking. "Today the government won. We took down the most ruthless cartel killer, Hernandez Prez. His brother is Deloso Prez of the cartel. He's serving four life sentences. So the city is safe once again. I'll take a few question now."

"Will there be any retaliation?"

"We will be ready if there is."

"So you said he got four life sentences?"

"Yes. That's correct."

"Are you scared for your life because you took down the cartel?"

"No."

"Is Deloso still in the city?"

"He never was."

"So you don't think they will try and blow your car up?"

Frank stepped to the mic. "Enough. Thank you."

"Baby, you were great as always." Bobby smiled.

"Thank you."

"You want to get some lunch?"

"Sure. Let me get my purse."

Back at my office, as I went to grab my purse, I saw a white envelope with my name on it. I stopped and opened it. I pulled out a letter that had red writing on it that said "YOU DEAD, BITCH!" My heart skipped a beat and my hands went to shaking.

Just then Bobby knocked on my door. I hurried up and slid the letter into my purse.

"You ready?"

"Yes."

"Is everything all right?"

"Yes, I'm fine. Let's go." I wasn't going to tell him about the letter. I didn't need him all up in my ass 24/7.

CHAPTER 36
Shantell
Six months later

After all the drama we had been through, we decided to move to Atlanta, but it would be a couple weeks before our house was finished getting built.

They had eventually found a lot of bodies buried around the warehouse. Deloso had been charged with dozens more murders. The Zetas Cartel had been fighting the Gulf Coast Cartel on the border and was winning. The U.S. had to send troops over to help out the Mexican government.

Keith's company had took off and he got the city contract for the hospital. Plus he had been spending a lot more time at the house once he found out I was pregnant.

I can't lie. I miss Darrell. He would be a great husband and father.

I haven't told Keith that it's someone else's baby. I'm not that fucking stupid. I know I had been pregnant for this man like three time. It might be meant for me to have this nigga's baby and to be with him. I had found out a week after me and Darrell had our one night stand. I decided that Keith and I were going to raise this child as our own. I know I'm down bad, but this my life. I'll live it like I wish. If there's consequences, I'll worry about that later.

I brought out dinner to the table. As we enjoyed a family dinner, I looked around at my family at the table and was happy. I had made a lot of mistakes. I lost my mother and my friends. But that's the price you pay when you're CAUGHT UP IN THE LIFE.

Robert Baptiste

CHAPTER 37
Darrell

As I pulled up to the house, I looked at Shantell's picture. I couldn't believe this dumb bitch was caught up in some shit with the cartel. She thought it was finished. She believed she and her bitch ass husband would live happily ever after. The shit doesn't work like that.

Keith should have known better. I don't know why he put his wife up to it since he knows the repercussions of this shit. I know the bitch said she had a secret, but I didn't know it was that big. The dumb bitch told on the head of a cartel. Now I had to come in and clean up.

I had been in New Orleans for several months. The dumb-ass Mexican Hernandez hired to do this fucked everything up. He had made shit hot. When I killed David Green, that shit was easy. No police. No questions. In and out.

I got out of the car and knocked on the door. I hate to kill some good pussy, but the bitch is not fucking with me anymore. I'd been looking for Keith, but the nigga hadn't been out of town. She'll do. Her and the kids. If they're at friends' houses, I'll do them after I do this bitch.

I knocked. Her head was going to be fucked up when she saw me.

She came down that stairs with her hair hanging long. I can't lie. The bitch turns me on every time I see her. It doesn't help the situation either. She fixed her red robe and looked through the glass door, but I turned my head.

She opened the door. I turned around, surprising her. Her eyes were as big as quarters. She looked like a dear caught in a headlight.

"Darrell, what are you doing here? How did you find where I lived? You can't be here."

"Why not?"

"You know why?"

"Because of your punk-ass husband."

"I told you it was over between us."

"I'm not concerned about this shit. Fuck him."

"How did you find me? I never told you were I stay."

"I got ways to find who I want to find."

"You've been stalking me?"

"Something like that."

"What?"

"Can I come in?"

"No."

"We need to talk."

"No, we don't. I think you should leave before my husband comes home."

"His punk-ass is in New Orleans."

"How do you know that?"

"I told you. I know things."

"You need leave for real. I'm calling the police."

She tried to close the door. I put my foot in it.

"Move your foot. Don't make me call the police on your ass."

"I told you that we need to talk."

"I'll get in trouble if my kids see you."

"They are out with friends." I shoved the door open.

She tried to run, but I grabbed her by the hair and threw her on the sofa. She tried to kick me. I punched her in the face. I pulled my gun and aimed it in her face.

"Please, Darrell."

"I told you before. Everybody has secrets. Mine is I'm an assassin for the cartel. I'm supposed to kill you."

"Please no."

"This is just business."

"I thought you loved me."

"Love has nothing to do with this. That shit's on the back burner. It's just business."

"Please. I have kids."

"They're next." I aimed my gun at her head.

"Darrell, I'm pregnant."

"What?"

"It's yours." I opened my robe and showed him my stomach.

"How do I know it mine?"

"I'm at four months. Do the math."

"Why haven't you told me?"

"I was moving on with my husband. I didn't know if I would keep it."

"Bitch, I should kill your trifling ass and that kid. Normally, I would. But I'm going to let you make it for now, but I'm going to kill your husband. If you weren't carrying my child, I'd kill you too."

"What about my kids?"

"I don't know. But your ass better keep me in the loop. If the baby isn't mine, you and your baby is dead." I walked out.

CHAPTER 38
Shantell

My heart was pounding in my chest. I felt just like I did when Keith threatened me. I couldn't believe Darrell was an assassin for the cartel. He was going to kill me for real. I saw it in his eyes.

I wondered how much of that shit he told me about his life was true. All that shit about his wife. He might not have even been married. He told me he had killed Dave Green.

Shit. I had forgotten about Keith. I called him, but the phone went to voicemail. "Please call back as soon as you get this. It's an emergency."

I threw on some clothes and drove to Taraji's. I needed to talk to her. I must have the worst luck in the fucking world.

I pounded on Taraji's door like I was the police. She opened the door and stared. My eyes were blood red and my hair was a mess.

"What's wrong? Why are you beating on my door at one a.m.?"

"I have to talk."

I barreled past her. I grabbed the remains of a blunt from her ashtray. I lit it and hit it hard. I knew it was bad for the baby, but I had to settle my nerves.

"Bitch, what's wrong? It better be life or death. I was sleeping good."

"Bitch, Darrell came to my house to kill me."

"Stop pacing and speak slower."

"You heard me. Darrell was going to kill me."

"I thought you broke it off with him."

"I did."

"How did he know you moved here?"

"This motherfucker is an assassin for the cartel."

She started laughing, "Bitch, you've been snorting too much. You've gotten paranoid."

"Look in my face. Good." I showed her the bruise on my face.

"Fuck. Bitch, you're not playing."

"Bitch, I'm stone serious."

"What did he say?"

"The cartel had a hit on me and my family. He was there to clean up."

"What?"

"The real punchline is… You better sit down, or you might hurt yourself laughing."

"What is it?"

"The real reason that nigga ain't killed my ass. Check this shit out."

"What? Bitch, spit it out."

I took another hit of the blunt. "You ready for this shit?"

"Bitch, come out with it."

"The baby I'm pregnant with is his."

"What the fuck did you just say?"

"I'm carrying his baby."

"You told me it was Keith's baby."

"I can't tell him it's for some else. But the truth is I was fucking both of them at the same time."

"Bitch, you're all fucked up."

"You think?"

"Let me get this straight. Your baby daddy wants to kill your whole family?"

"Yes. He's going to kill Keith."

"Did you warn him?"

"I've called a lot, but it always goes to voicemail. He's in New Orleans."

"Bitch, I thought this was all over when you killed Deloso's brother?"

"Me too. But it's not."

"That witness program don't sound too bad now.

"Fuck! Fuck! My life is all fucked up."

"You can say that shit again. I just wanted my husband out of jail. I didn't ask for all this other shit. I should have left his ass in there."

192

"Don't say that."
"My life is flipped upside down."
"I see."
I began to cry.
"I'll always be here for you."
I dialed Keith's number. "Fuck!" It went to voicemail.

Robert Baptiste

CHAPTER 39
Darrell

I drove around New Orleans looking for that nigga. He wasn't at his house. I had people watching it. When I find him, his life is over. I can't let him make it. I was serious about the kid with Shantell. If it wasn't mine, I was killing both of them. I'm letting her make it…if it's my baby. I can't kill my own kid.

My wife and I always wanted a baby, but she died before we had one. We never had a chance. But now, I may have one. Once I killed this nigga, I'd take Shantell and we'll go away. If Deloso finds out she's still alive he'll kill her, the baby, and me.

My phone rang. I winced when I saw it was Deloso.

"Have you killed the bitch and her husband yet?"

"Not yet."

"What are you waiting for?"

"I haven't found her yet. I think she moved, maybe to Atlanta. But I'm on Keith's trail as we speak."

"Make it happen. Sooner rather than later. Kill everyone."

"I'm on it "

"Don't bring your ass back to Texas without handling this business. They killed my brother and ratted on me. They have to pay for it."

"Got you."

That bitch had put me in a hell of a bind with the cartel.

I looked up and saw Keith pull up to a condo in Slidell. His company owned it. It was show time.

Robert Baptiste

CHAPTER 40
Keith

I got back in town from Atlanta. I had linked the deal with the city to help build downtown. After all the drama in the city. It was time for me to move on. I had worn out my welcome in New Orleans. I was a city to have fun in, but not to live in. I had done too much dirt. I had too much pain. It was time for me to move on.

I pulled up to my sister's house because I hadn't seen her in a couple months and she had been crying for me to come kick with her, especially after I got out of the hospital. She still didn't know the true story and I wasn't going to tell her because she would want to kill Shantell's ass for real. And plus I need her to run my company in New Orleans for me. I can't let just anybody take over it.

I really needed to send more time with my family, especially since Shantell was pregnant.

I saw that I had a bunch of messages and missed calls from Shantell. I prayed that the baby was all right. I was dialing her number as I heard a shot.

I felt a burning pain deep in my chest. I saw the man with a gun, but I couldn't do anything about it. Glass shattered and covered my face and chest. I was laying there with my eyes wide open. I knew this shit with the cartel wasn't over.

My life passed before me. There were moments of great ugliness. People I had killed and tortured. There was also great beauty. Shantell on our wedding day. The birth of our kids.

I heard my mother's voice. "Baby boy, you got to pay for the things you do. The past always has way of catching up with you."

Everything went black. My soul seemed to lift from my body.

"Sir, hold on, everything is under control."

I wanted to tell her it was too late.

I wished I could tell Keith Jr. and Ka'wine how much I loved them and that I was proud of them. I wanted to see my new kid born. I guess it wasn't in the cards.

I flat lined.

They pumped on my chest as they tried to bring me back.
I thought about how I got in the game in the beginning...

To Be Continued...

Submission Guideline

Submit the first three chapters of your completed manuscript to ldpsubmissions@gmail.com, subject line: Your book's title. The manuscript must be in a .doc file and sent as an attachment. Document should be in Times New Roman, double spaced and in size 12 font. Also, provide your synopsis and full contact information. If sending multiple submissions, they must each be in a separate email.

Have a story but no way to send it electronically? You can still submit to LDP/Ca$h Presents. Send in the first three chapters, written or typed, of your completed manuscript to:

LDP: Submissions Dept
Po Box 944
Stockbridge, Ga 30281

DO NOT send original manuscript. Must be a duplicate.

Provide your synopsis and a cover letter containing your full contact information.

Thanks for considering LDP and Ca$h Presents.

Coming Soon from Lock Down Publications/Ca$h Presents

BOW DOWN TO MY GANGSTA
By **Ca$h**
TORN BETWEEN TWO
By **Coffee**
THE STREETS STAINED MY SOUL **II**
By **Marcellus Allen**
BLOOD OF A BOSS **VI**
SHADOWS OF THE GAME II
By **Askari**
LOYAL TO THE GAME **IV**
By **T.J. & Jelissa**
A DOPEBOY'S PRAYER **II**
By **Eddie "Wolf" Lee**
IF LOVING YOU IS WRONG… **III**
By **Jelissa**
TRUE SAVAGE **VII**
MIDNIGHT CARTEL III
DOPE BOY MAGIC IV
By **Chris Green**
BLAST FOR ME **III**
A SAVAGE DOPEBOY III
CUTTHROAT MAFIA II
By **Ghost**
A HUSTLER'S DECEIT III
KILL ZONE **II**
BAE BELONGS TO ME III
A DOPE BOY'S QUEEN II
By **Aryanna**

CHAINED TO THE STREETS III
By **J-Blunt**
COKE KINGS V
KING OF THE TRAP II
By **T.J. Edwards**
GORILLAZ IN THE BAY V
TEARS OF A GANGSTA II
De'Kari
THE STREETS ARE CALLING II
Duquie Wilson
KINGPIN KILLAZ IV
STREET KINGS III
PAID IN BLOOD III
CARTEL KILLAZ IV
DOPE GODS II
Hood Rich
SINS OF A HUSTLA II
ASAD
TRIGGADALE III
Elijah R. Freeman
KINGZ OF THE GAME V
Playa Ray
SLAUGHTER GANG IV
RUTHLESS HEART IV
By Willie Slaughter
THE HEART OF A SAVAGE III
By Jibril Williams
FUK SHYT II
By Blakk Diamond
THE DOPEMAN'S BODYGAURD II

Robert Baptiste

By Tranay Adams
TRAP GOD II
By Troublesome
YAYO III
A SHOOTER'S AMBITION III
By S. Allen
GHOST MOB
Stilloan Robinson
KINGPIN DREAMS II
By Paper Boi Rari
CREAM
By Yolanda Moore
SON OF A DOPE FIEND II
By Renta
FOREVER GANGSTA II
GLOCKS ON SATIN SHEETS II
By Adrian Dulan
LOYALTY AIN'T PROMISED II
By Keith Williams
THE PRICE YOU PAY FOR LOVE II
DOPE GIRL MAGIC II
By Destiny Skai
CONFESSIONS OF A GANGSTA II
By Nicholas Lock
I'M NOTHING WITHOUT HIS LOVE II
By Monet Dragun
CAUGHT UP IN THE LIFE III
By Robert Baptiste
NEW TO THE GAME III
By **Malik D. Rice**

LIFE OF A SAVAGE III

By **Romell Tukes**

QUIET MONEY II

By **Trai'Quan**

THE STREETS MADE ME II

By **Larry D. Wright**

THE ULTIMATE SACRIFICE VI

By **Anthony Fields**

THE LIFE OF A HOOD STAR

By **Ca$h & Rashia Wilson**

Available Now

RESTRAINING ORDER **I & II**

By **CA$H & Coffee**

LOVE KNOWS NO BOUNDARIES **I II & III**

By **Coffee**

RAISED AS A GOON I, II, III & IV

BRED BY THE SLUMS I, II, III

BLAST FOR ME I & II

ROTTEN TO THE CORE I II III

A BRONX TALE I, II, III

DUFFEL BAG CARTEL I II III IV

HEARTLESS GOON I II III IV

A SAVAGE DOPEBOY I II

HEARTLESS GOON I II III

DRUG LORDS I II III

CUTTHROAT MAFIA

Robert Baptiste

By **Ghost**
LAY IT DOWN **I & II**
LAST OF A DYING BREED
BLOOD STAINS OF A SHOTTA I & II III
By **Jamaica**
LOYAL TO THE GAME I II III
LIFE OF SIN I, II III
By **TJ & Jelissa**
BLOODY COMMAS I & II
SKI MASK CARTEL I II & III
KING OF NEW YORK I II,III IV V
RISE TO POWER I II III
COKE KINGS I II III IV
BORN HEARTLESS I II III IV
KING OF THE TRAP
By **T.J. Edwards**
IF LOVING HIM IS WRONG…I & II
LOVE ME EVEN WHEN IT HURTS I II III
By **Jelissa**
WHEN THE STREETS CLAP BACK I & II III
THE HEART OF A SAVAGE I II
By **Jibril Williams**
A DISTINGUISHED THUG STOLE MY HEART I II & III
LOVE SHOULDN'T HURT I II III IV
RENEGADE BOYS I II III IV
PAID IN KARMA I II III
By **Meesha**
A GANGSTER'S CODE I &, II III
A GANGSTER'S SYN I II III
THE SAVAGE LIFE I II III

Caught Up in the Life 2

CHAINED TO THE STREETS I II
By J-Blunt
PUSH IT TO THE LIMIT
By **Bre' Hayes**
BLOOD OF A BOSS **I, II, III, IV, V**
SHADOWS OF THE GAME
By **Askari**
THE STREETS BLEED MURDER **I, II & III**
THE HEART OF A GANGSTA I II& III
By **Jerry Jackson**
CUM FOR ME I II III IV V
An **LDP Erotica Collaboration**
BRIDE OF A HUSTLA **I II & II**
THE FETTI GIRLS **I, II& III**
CORRUPTED BY A GANGSTA I, II III, IV
BLINDED BY HIS LOVE
THE PRICE YOU PAY FOR LOVE
DOPE GIRL MAGIC
By **Destiny Skai**
WHEN A GOOD GIRL GOES BAD
By **Adrienne**
THE COST OF LOYALTY I II III
By Kweli
A GANGSTER'S REVENGE **I II III & IV**
THE BOSS MAN'S DAUGHTERS I II III IV V
A SAVAGE LOVE **I & II**
BAE BELONGS TO ME I II
A HUSTLER'S DECEIT I, II, III
WHAT BAD BITCHES DO I, II, III
SOUL OF A MONSTER I II III

KILL ZONE

A DOPE BOY'S QUEEN

By **Aryanna**

A KINGPIN'S AMBITON

A KINGPIN'S AMBITION **II**

I MURDER FOR THE DOUGH

By **Ambitious**

TRUE SAVAGE I II III IV V VI

DOPE BOY MAGIC I, II, III

MIDNIGHT CARTEL I II

By **Chris Green**

A DOPEBOY'S PRAYER

By **Eddie "Wolf" Lee**

THE KING CARTEL **I, II & III**

By **Frank Gresham**

THESE NIGGAS AIN'T LOYAL **I, II & III**

By **Nikki Tee**

GANGSTA SHYT **I II &III**

By **CATO**

THE ULTIMATE BETRAYAL

By **Phoenix**

BOSS'N UP **I , II & III**

By **Royal Nicole**

I LOVE YOU TO DEATH

By Destiny J

I RIDE FOR MY HITTA

I STILL RIDE FOR MY HITTA

By **Misty Holt**

LOVE & CHASIN' PAPER

By **Qay Crockett**

TO DIE IN VAIN
SINS OF A HUSTLA
By **ASAD**
BROOKLYN HUSTLAZ
By **Boogsy Morina**
BROOKLYN ON LOCK I & II
By **Sonovia**
GANGSTA CITY
By **Teddy Duke**
A DRUG KING AND HIS DIAMOND I & II III
A DOPEMAN'S RICHES
HER MAN, MINE'S TOO I, II
CASH MONEY HO'S
By Nicole Goosby
TRAPHOUSE KING **I II & III**
KINGPIN KILLAZ I II III
STREET KINGS I II
PAID IN BLOOD **I II**
CARTEL KILLAZ I II III
DOPE GODS
By **Hood Rich**
LIPSTICK KILLAH **I, II, III**
CRIME OF PASSION I II & III
By **Mimi**
STEADY MOBBN' **I, II, III**
THE STREETS STAINED MY SOUL
By **Marcellus Allen**
WHO SHOT YA **I, II, III**
SON OF A DOPE FIEND
Renta

Robert Baptiste

GORILLAZ IN THE BAY **I II III IV**

TEARS OF A GANGSTA

DE'KARI

TRIGGADALE I II

Elijah R. Freeman

GOD BLESS THE TRAPPERS I, II, III

THESE SCANDALOUS STREETS I, II, III

FEAR MY GANGSTA I, II, III

THESE STREETS DON'T LOVE NOBODY I, II

BURY ME A G I, II, III, IV, V

A GANGSTA'S EMPIRE I, II, III, IV

THE DOPEMAN'S BODYGAURD

Tranay Adams

THE STREETS ARE CALLING

Duquie Wilson

MARRIED TO A BOSS… I II III

By Destiny Skai & Chris Green

KINGZ OF THE GAME I II III IV

Playa Ray

SLAUGHTER GANG I II III

RUTHLESS HEART I II III

By Willie Slaughter

FUK SHYT

By Blakk Diamond

DON'T F#CK WITH MY HEART I II

By Linnea

ADDICTED TO THE DRAMA I II III

By Jamila

YAYO I II

A SHOOTER'S AMBITION I II

By S. Allen

TRAP GOD

By Troublesome

FOREVER GANGSTA

GLOCKS ON SATIN SHEETS

By Adrian Dulan

TOE TAGZ I II III

By Ah'Million

KINGPIN DREAMS

By Paper Boi Rari

CONFESSIONS OF A GANGSTA

By Nicholas Lock

I'M NOTHING WITHOUT HIS LOVE

By Monet Dragun

CAUGHT UP IN THE LIFE I II

By Robert Baptiste

NEW TO THE GAME I II

By **Malik D. Rice**

Life of a Savage I II

By **Romell Tukes**

LOYALTY AIN'T PROMISED

By Keith Williams

Quiet Money

By **Trai'Quan**

THE STREETS MADE ME

By **Larry D. Wright**

THE ULTIMATE SACRIFICE I, II, III, IV, V

KHADIFI

By **Anthony Fields**

THE LIFE OF A HOOD STAR

Robert Baptiste

By Ca$h & Rashia Wilson

BOOKS BY LDP'S CEO, CA$H

TRUST IN NO MAN

TRUST IN NO MAN 2

TRUST IN NO MAN 3

BONDED BY BLOOD

SHORTY GOT A THUG

THUGS CRY

THUGS CRY 2

THUGS CRY 3

TRUST NO BITCH

TRUST NO BITCH 2

TRUST NO BITCH 3

TIL MY CASKET DROPS

RESTRAINING ORDER

RESTRAINING ORDER 2

IN LOVE WITH A CONVICT

LIFE OF A HOOD STAR

Coming Soon

BONDED BY BLOOD 2

BOW DOWN TO MY GANGSTA

Robert Baptiste

CPSIA information can be obtained
at www.ICGtesting.com
Printed in the USA
LVHW081812281020
670068LV00011B/1251